HUGGING THISTLES

Hugging Thistles

Aideen Henry

HUGGING THISTLES

is published in 2013 by
ARLEN HOUSE
42 Grange Abbey Road
Baldoyle
Dublin 13
Ireland
Phone/Fax: 353 86 8207617
Email: arlenhouse@gmail.com
arlenhouse.blogspot.com

Distributed internationally by
SYRACUSE UNIVERSITY PRESS
621 Skytop Road, Suite 110
Syracuse, NY 13244–5290
Phone: 315–443–5534/Fax: 315–443–5545
Email: supress@syr.edu

978–1–85132–047–9, paperback
978–1–85132–067–7, hardback

Typesetting ¦ Arlen House
Lithographic Printing ¦ Brunswick Press
Front Cover ¦ 'Seasonal' by Angela O'Brien
Back Cover ¦ 'Waning' by Helen Caird
for further information please contact helen.caird@gmail.com

Contents

ACKNOWLEDGEMENTS

Thanks are due to the editors of the following publications where some of these stories first appeared:

'Idling' in *The Dublin Review*.
'Flock Memory' in *Wordlegs*.
'Antemortem' in *Town of Fiction* (Atlantis Collective, 2009).
'Oculoterra' and 'Shapeshifter' in *Faceless Monsters* (Atlantis Collective, 2010).
'A Kind of a Smothering' and 'Blind Spot' in *Eat the Swans* (Atlantis Collective, 2011).

'Oculoterra' was selected for the inaugural Lonely Voice Series at the Irish Writers' Centre reading in January 2010.

'Saibh' and 'Idling' were shortlisted for the Francis MacManus Award in 2011 and 2012 respectively.

Special thanks to the writers in the Atlantis Collective for their astute editorial assistance: Colm Brady, Alan Caden, Trish Holmes, Conor Montague, Dara Ó Foghlú, Máire T. Robinson.

Thanks also to Enniskillen Library and South West College for the generous use of their library facilities.

Hugging Thistles

Oculoterra

Kieran's home is full of traps, things forgotten, like homework and brushing teeth. Giving the wrong answers to questions, like 'Do you think I'm an idiot?' or 'You don't really hate your sister, do you?' Always obstacles to overcome before he can reach the good stuff.

'Four more weeks of not cursing and Dr Octavius will be mine'.

Kieran sticks out his tongue, pulls down his lower lids so they look like his grandfather's bloodshot droopy eyes and in a gravelly voice says:

'You're a grand little fecker. Aren't you?'

He flushes the toilet, sniffs his fingers and lets the tap run as if he is washing his hands. He needs longer thumbnails to open knots on his fishing line. Pulling the navy towel off the wooden rail, he wraps it, scarf-like, around his head. In his mother's no-time-for-any-of-your-crap face, he squishes his nose against the mirror and screws up his eyes so they bulge like two black golf balls.

'You're just like your father, you little bleep, selfish to the bleep, and all I bleeping do for you'.

Kieran's real home is a faintly visible satellite of the moon, best seen on a cold, clear November evening; Oculoterra is a freckle in the white of the eye of the dying moon. There, his mother is a warm bath that never overheats or cools. He steps in and out of her whenever he pleases. He bathes in her while he sleeps. And even when he leaves, he can still smell her like perfume on the inside of his wrists. His father is a talking goalpost. When Kieran scores, his father cheers and tells him how many miles an hour each ball travels and the odds ratio of Gawky Lydon saving it. Kieran's sister is the jittery feeling he gets when jumping off the top diving board or catching his first mackerel on his new three line hook, on a wet summer's evening.

He closes the bathroom door behind him, switches off the fan and lip-syncs his mother as she shouts:

'Did you flush and switch off the fan?'

He sprints out the door, the tips of his new football boots gripping the lino. The door slams behind him, shaking its frame. He slows down as he gets to the green. Jonathan, a fair-haired boy with a cowlick and brown eyes, is driving the go-kart his father built for him, with PJ standing on the back. PJ is tall with buck-teeth and matchstick legs. Kieran stands on the kerb, chewing the cuff of his sleeve, staring after them and then at his boots. They approach him and spin the go-kart with a handbrake turn causing him to jump back.

'What's with the gammy boots, Kieran?' Jonathan says.

'Want to play football?'

'Are we playing football, PJ', says Jonathan, imitating his voice, 'with this retard?'

PJ giggles, his lips uncovering a gummy smile. They speed away, Jonathan shouting back,

'Try the Brazilians, gay boy, they're always up for it'.

Kieran watches them leave the estate and joins Romero and Juan on the next green, relieved they don't speak English, just football.

Mornings in Oculoterra are spent building go-karts from the royal architect's plans. Each go-kart has a detachable throne with a self-inflating balloon to the rear and pedal steering on the front wheels. Kieran leads the trail of go-karts down the burnt-orange track that runs into the purple helium sea. The trick is to pull the cord just before the front wheels hit the gassy water. The go-kart launches into the air suspended from its balloon; he spends hours gliding and tumbling, rolling and sliding in the thick air over Oculo Bay. His balloon is a playful puppy. It refuels by diving into the bubbling bay then blows him out of the water like whale spray. He takes turns to lead and be led in the dance with the balloon. When he tires, the balloon swings around and scoops him up like a giant palm, his hands and feet spilling over the sides. It carries him back to his cushioned pod in the palace where he naps. When he wakes, a book opens and reads itself to him while his eyes fix on the clouds of taffeta out the window. There are no rules so he can pick his nose, curse or hold his willy whenever he pleases. There is no school so no need to plot skirmishes or counter attacks against Jonathon in the yard. No bruised shins or scratchy lice either.

Kieran sleeps in the box room. If he lies on his bed with his arms overhead, his fingertips can touch one wall while his toes touch the other. Chelsea footballers adorn his wardrobe door. Stuck to his mirror are pictures of toy warriors that can be twisted to make cars or tanks. By his bedside is a box of all his scary plastic characters from wrestling, *Batman* and *Harry Potter*. He just needs Dr Octavius to complete the set. His mother has called him twice for school but he has a few more minutes before the high-pitched screech. The one she uses when she really means it.

Just as his face finds a cool part of the pillow to rest on, she surprises him with her sudden weight on his bed. She never comes into his room. She looks around like the way he does at the aquarium when he watches turtles stroke the water. Something's up. She's not screaming. She's not in her there-could-be-ten-mammies-in-there dressing-gown. She's wearing her very-important perfume and using her serious conversation voice. Fuck. She starts stroking his face. Must be bad. She starts talking in grown-up duck and dive. She is staring at the duvet, her left eye blinking while her right stays open, glazed. He looks over her shoulder at Ronaldinho, waiting it out. Bet he wouldn't talk and talk like this. Just speaks with his feet. Kieran waits for the meaning. It usually follows after a pause, a deep breath and a 'So …'. Here it is.

'So, we have decided that it's best for everyone if your father moves out'.

'He's Dad. Don't call him "your father". Why? What happened anyway?'

'But I've just explained, dear'.

She has that patient look she gives the really thick kids she teaches in her remedial class. Kieran used to sit into her 'special' class when he finished school an hour early in Babies. Why do they call them special anyway? They're just thick or not listening. Then he has a terrible thought and starts crying.

'Ah, now, now. What is it?' she rubs his cheek.

'My friends'll think my Dad's gay'.

'Now why would you say that?'

'He'll dress like a girl and we'll never see him'.

The moment of sweet sadness when his mother holds both his cheeks in the palms of her hands and looks deep into his eyes is broken by Sly Susan, his sister, slithering at the door.

'He's getting Tootsie crossed with Mary Poppins. Poor kid'.

His mother laughs, then checks herself when she sees his face. 'Ah, Kieran. You'll see your father every weekend'.

'– So how long is it for, anyway?'

His mother and Sly exchange looks.

'It's for the moment. For the time being'.

Sly moves into his room, draws back her hair, ties it in a ponytail, stands in side view to the mirror admiring her new breasts and her high curved bum.

'Out', Kieran roars. 'Out of my room. Now! I want to get dressed'.

'Well, isn't that good to hear!' says his mother, standing up. Sly smirks as she slopes out.

In the evenings, after marbles, he goes hunting or fishing. Hunting is great because it is real. He can choose whom he will hunt and they always show up. He carries one spear while two Irish wolfhounds, Fite and Fuaite, carry spares on their backs in leather harnesses. The forest is a breathable green liquid he swims through, undulating his body, head first, his spear at his side. The trees are black seaweed with eel-like leaves and branches moving like hair under water. When he spots his prey he shouts:

'Halt!' They freeze. Then he shoots them. The spears pinch as they go through, like needles through silk, then return to his hand until his prey says the magic words.

'Kieran, you are king. I am your humble servant'.

Sometimes his prey is so thick he has to give them hints. The boys are quicker than the girls. The girls screech at him not to touch them. As if.

Once they have said the magic words their pinprick wounds re-seal, they unfreeze and he can go on hunting. Sometimes he hunts the same person all evening. Other times he goes fishing.

This broken-home craic is pretty good; his father does stuff with him on Saturday and Sunday afternoons now, like going to football matches and teaching him how to play pool. And his mother rubs him on the head and on the backs of his shoulders more. Her hugs last longer too. Sly has wangled an iPod out of Dad. She just has to sulk and say:

'I'm having a bad time at school'.

Dad's chin puckers and his eyes look over their heads to the place where their family was before it broke up. Kieran doesn't care as long as Dr Octavius is on the way.

On Saturday afternoon Kieran stands as usual outside HMV. He looks at the beams of white light shining up at the sky from glass discs in the ground. He wonders are they lights coming from an underworld where all is bright and cheerful and where scatters of light escape through its sieve-like roof into the floor of his grey day. Dad's late. He's smiling too much, leering and slurry too. He smells bad as he presses his lips to Kieran's forehead. Kieran ducks away from him, checking no one has seen. They go to the big screen in Fitzers and Kieran sips a coke. Dad is scary. He stares at the wall below the screen and doesn't seem to hear Kieran when he tells him he has to leave early.

Kieran runs home, not stopping as he usually does to peg stones at the upturned Tesco trolley in the canal. There's a blue BMW in the driveway with a baby seat in the back. In the kitchen there's a big thing sitting in Dad's seat. It's got a wide face, too many teeth, sticky short hair and shiny tanned skin. It's got its hairy paw on his mother's bottom as she stands beside it. His mother jumps when she sees Kieran. The thing starts talking,

'Delighted ... wonderful ... super!'

Spit flies out of its mouth, landing on Dad's armrest. Kieran watches a ladybird walk over the back of his father's chair. After the thing's paw has mussed Kieran's hair, the same paw that was on his mother's bottom, it sits back in Dad's chair again, its mouth still making lots of noises. Kieran's mother makes tea, glancing from Kieran to the thing and back, pretend-smiling. Kieran escapes out to the clothesline with a basket of wet laundry. He grabs his sister's iPod from the key hook on the way out and connects the earphones.

He stretches the heavy cotton towels taut, overlapping two corners under each peg, while looking in the kitchen window. His mother is jumpier, all girly. He can see Sly in her. Her clothes are different. Kieran gives every pair of sockwoks and briary a peg each. He stretches two cardrigeens over three pegs. His underpunders look lonely so he puts two to a peg. From behind the sheets he spies on the thing again. It's wide, not tall. It has tree trunk legs and swirls of hair on its bare arms, with tufts creeping over the top of its shirt collar. Maybe it has goat's legs. Kieran wonders what its roar is like.

His mother looks nervous as it paws her again then it takes its covering from the coat hook, sticks its tongue in his mother's mouth and leaves. Kieran stands over the empty basket, his two hands on the washing line holding it below eye level. Behind the sheet his Adam's apple moves up and down. He has nothing to swallow. He looks up at the grey sky. Cloud covers it like a crochet skullcap; fluffy holes of blue visible through it here and there. A mournful love song plays in the middle of his head, pulsating in the soft flesh of his chest and stomach.

'Fuck. Fuck. Fuck'. he says.

He kicks the empty wash basket against the wall and runs inside and upstairs to his bedroom, locking the door. He pulls out the earphones and throws himself face down on his bed.

The best place to fish is Lake Gratitude. His line has a hook the size of a clenched fist. There are no fish in the lake but he always catches something. He stands astride the limestone shelf and whips his rod until his line shimmies across to the centre of the lake. There it drops deep, making the sound of a coin landing in an empty tin can. He begins to reel it in. Sometimes objects like a leather handbag or a white car surface. Other times a fur hat or a velvet couch. Each object looks around for him and rushes to tell its story.

'I belonged to a woman once who ...'

Every story is different but they all have the same pattern; something awful has happened to each of the owners. Once the story is told the object submerges again. Kieran can ask it two questions before it disappears. He always asks the same two.

'What football team did your owner support?'

And, 'Did he or she have beautiful hands?'

Once the object has answered it submerges again, the water closing over it like a plate of glass. Then the sound of a clacking sewing machine fills the air.

Saibh

Saibh tends to fall in love with men she doesn't like. It is a gradual process. Some aspect repels her. With James, his arrogance, Seán, his tendency to snort, Wojciech, his loud aftershave. And his age. Once the man has moved from her eligible category to her definitely-not category, he is outside her radar. This is a dangerous place. She is kind and thoughtful to such men, treating them like girlfriends. Her guard is down. She is herself. Gradually she loses sight of the repelling feature and finds herself falling into them.

In time she describes a fondness for 'his cute ears' or 'his awful jackets', protective of the very feature that put her off in the first place. Once the in-lovedness wears off however, she returns to her starting position, collecting her original dislike on her way out.

In contrast, she is wary of men she finds attractive. They could not live up to her expectations so better to carry them in her imagination and daydream about their perfection rather than discover in what way they fall short. Since Valentin was born she can't imagine falling in love with any man again.

She sits at a formica table where the finger prints and crumbs from the last occupant are still visible on its greasy surface. She is slight in frame, long limbed and slender fingered. She finishes her coffee and examines the pastries on display, aware of her right breast slowly refilling and her left breast brimming. The bakery is in a market town, on the rail link an hour from what is now home. These towns are all alike. The bakery or café is the social hub for those with no work to go to. A young man in the corner shakes as he rolls a cigarette. A mother with two young children looks out the window into the overcast day. An unemployed older man busies himself with his newspaper, folding it carefully into quarters as he reads each section. The woman behind the counter raises her eyebrows at Saibh; her hair is trapped in a white net and her pink uniform strains across her chest.

'I'll have the cream slice, the coffee one, with a second cup of coffee, please'.

'Righteo'.

Sugar sticks to the roof of her mouth, like communion before it moistens. Puff pastry crumbles between her teeth and a blob of cream lolls on her tongue. She savours the pastry, focussing her eyes just in front of her plate. With effort she can make her eyes see darkness while still remaining open and bring her attention to the textures in her mouth. She daren't close her eyes. She licks her finger to mop up the last flaky crumbs. Mother never allowed cream cakes.

The bell over the shop door rings when she leaves the bakery. Further down the street in a charity shop, she selects a Mills & Boon from the second-hand stall. Looking through the belts and dishes, she keeps expecting to find her mother's things. The golden hairbrush and mirror with long tarnished handles. The treasured fur coat. The trinkets collected from each foreign holiday, from a time when she still left the house. Saibh felt like someone else when she cleared out that house. As though she were standing beside herself, telling herself what she should do next.

'Now, you will put all her clothes into these boxes'.

The voice sounded so sure of itself. She even asked it questions.

'What about her fur coat? She really cherished that. And her jewellery and knickknacks?'

'She did. But you didn't, did you? No. So into the box with it all. You won't have to always look your best when you go out or hear anymore about how great the Clancy's daughter is doing in London now, will you? No'.

The part of her packing her mother's things acquiesced. It wasn't as strong as this other self which seemed to understand the world, seemed to know her and what was best for her. Where did it come from? And where did it go to later? It knew that she shouldn't live on in her mother's house, that she didn't belong there. It knew that it was best to clear all personal things and to let the house until it was sold. It also knew that she should not be alone that night. It brought her by the hand down to the pub. It sat her down with a hot port and started her talking to Wojciech. It linked her arm to his as they walked, and led her to his bed. Wojciech was the kind of man her mother would have dissaproved of. A former olympian weight-lifter, he was a short wide man, fifteen years her senior. Oil was ingrained in the creases of his hands even after a long bath.

He stayed awake that night watching her. He was baffled to find this sylph-like creature lying next to him, with her blond hair tied in a low ponytail and her slender boyish hips. He thought of his estranged wife and two sons in Poland and how in the five years he had been in Ireland, he had not moved country until this night. He had found home, here in this strange child-woman, here in this bed.

The day following her mother's funeral, Saibh felt alone for the first time. She waited to conjure up that other part of herself that knew what to do, but could not reach it. She stepped in the door of her bedsit on the second floor of an old victorian house and removed her shoes. She peeled off her clothes and dropped onto her mattress on the floor for a nap. She felt a lack, a miss. She awoke from a dream in which she was kneeling inside her own transparent body, a giant hollow perspex sculpture. Piece by piece she was applying thumbnail-sized gold leaf to the inside of her body. Like a layering a collage. She was colouring herself in.

After a bath she sat in the window seat looking out at the pink cherry blossom petals stuck to the droplets on the window. She felt neutered to sentience, cauterised. Though still on compassionate leave, she dressed and dropped the keys and file of her mother's house to the auctioneers and went to work. The factory was noisy and she felt relieved to gown up, put in her earplugs and start work in the sealing room. She was the only staff member who chose to work alone in that room. The others working with noisy machinery attached their earphones to iPods or to the radio. Saibh loved the silence cupped inside her earplugs. She felt it held her in, she felt minded. As though her thoughts were harnessed, concentrated and sheltered. As though her brain was hugged. Like the way a magnifying glass focuses the multidirectional rays of the sun down onto one small area. She went into a trance. Work was a dance, a rythmic movement she liked; squat to lift an empty box, gather the assembled parts and stack in the box in order of size. Press the machine down on the lid to seal. Push the box along onto the belt. Next.

At lunchtime she sat next to Cynthia. Saibh's reserve contrasted with Cynthia's exuberance, much as how a thin girl often benefits from the backdrop of a fat friend. In return the fat friend receives more attention. The staff were hushed until they gave her the mass card. Then Cynthia regaled the group with her most recent gossip. Saibh sat quiet, wishing she could insert her earphones again.

That Friday night she went to the cinema with Wojciech and stayed over at his apartment. Their conversations were limited by his poor english and her reluctance to speak. Their communication took the form of a kindness to each other in their exchange of words and a gentle physicality.

Weeks passed and seeing Wojciech became her new normal. She had been feeling queezy and sleeping poorly since her mother's funeral so she did not realise she was pregnant until she went to the doctor wondering if she had worms, her stomach swollen and mobile with the flickering sensation of life.

Wojciech danced her around the room cheering in Polish at the news. He insisted she move in with him. She gave up her bedsit and moved her few things into the spare room of his ground floor apartment. He was excited enough for them both. He spent time preparing the baby's room, painting the walls and planing wood for a crib.

After baby Valentin was born, Saibh's job was reduced to a three-day week. She continued to leave the apartment at the usual time each day however and dropped Valentin off at the creche. Her trips out of town started on her free days. She felt herself led by the hand by that other part of her, accompanied to and from each town by it, but never clear on the purpose of any journey.

On the train home, Saibh removes the Mills & Boon from her bag and stares at the cover. A handsome doctor, flanked by two nurses, looks out at her; one nurse looks at him directly, the other coyly. She closes her eyes, leans her head back and lets the vibration of the train carry her for a few moments. The train stops momentarily. Out of the window she sees gold and yellow leaves flutter in the wind on a pile of stones turned black by the rainshower. The leaves look like material flowers sewn onto a child's dress. She looks down. Her breasts have doubled in size and there's a half-hour left to the journey. She stands and feels them bursting. In the toilet using a hand pump, she pumps six ounces of milk into a container. She looks in the mirror, her pale face sidelit by the window. She was never close to her mother. She expected to become so once she'd had a child.

Her route home walking from the station takes her past her old bedsit. She steps inside the gates and leans her back against the copper beech hedge. This holds her weight and hides her from the street. She feels the branches poking her through the material of her coat. Some leaves unload their cupped droplets down her neck. The lights in the bedsit are switched off. On other days she has seen a young man's shadow pass the window. She wonders does he walk around the bedsit naked as she once did, lying on the floor mattress, looking up through the tall windows at the sky and the cherry blossom branch tips that tap the window in the breeze. She looks across the garden as a blue-black raven lifts off from the bird table. On the free edge of each opening wing its feathers spread like fingers. Maybe happiness is something you only know about afterwards.

It is dark when she reaches home. Through the dining room window she sees the fire blazing. Valentin is in his high chair, sucking on his yellow duck and waving a green plastic spoon in the air. Saibh watches from the shadow, a light drizzle powdering her face. Wojciech places the baby's dinner on the table and sits next to him. Firelight shines on Wojciech's bare shoulders and arms, an aging Hercules beside the baby. He delivers spoonfuls of food from a height down to Valentin's open mouth. The baby's legs kick straight and his hands slap the table so it is with difficulty that each spoonful reaches its target.

Wojciech sees Saibh's face in the mirror. Through the window pane streaming with rain, her face looks transparent. Who is this woman, the mother of his son, more dilute, more distant since she moved in with him? He doesn't turn to face her. Her image retreats into the black. He hears her key turn in the lock and her call from the hall.

'I'm home'.

Valentin calls out and arches his back out of the seat as Saibh comes into the room smiling.

DEADLIGHTS

Úna slams the fridge door.

'Jesus, Ma, no orange juice. Fuck's sake. I need orange juice'.

She turns to face her mother, her long black hair flops in a plait over her shoulder. The outline of her breasts distorts the Care Bear on her long t-shirt. The t-shirt covers one shoulder and reaches her mid-thighs. She stretches to the top cupboard for cereal, revealing the curve of her slim buttock cheeks, nominally clad in skimpy underpants. Úna pads barefoot back to the table, slouches into her seat and munches cereal, her chin close to the bowl, and her eyes staring straight ahead. Her streaked mascara outlines the contours of her high cheekbones.

Marguerite, a barrel-shaped woman with dark roots in blond hair, looks up from the sink and watches her daughter slurp her breakfast. As she bends to scrub a saucepan she speaks lightly and quickly so the words have to be chased after to be heard.

'You might cover yourself up a bit better, young lady'.

'Ah, sure I live here, don't I?' Úna speaks through her food, flakes of cereal escaping her lower lip. 'Can I not let my hair down at home?'

'You don't see me gallivanting around the house half-naked'.

Úna glances at the broad backside of her mother and smiles.

'Is that fella here?' comes the voice from the sink.

'And who might that fella be, Ma?'

'Your consort. Your young man'.

Robert, a thin youth with gelled hair, enters the kitchen as though summoned. He stands at the door looking at Úna, his head hung forwards on his thin white neck. Úna flicks her head to one side towards a seat. He sits on his hands and looks at her in a vulnerable way. She musses his hair until he pulls away. Marguerite turns around.

'Oh, hello Robert. I didn't see you come in. Will you have some breakfast? Úna'll look after you'.

Robert squirms.

'Ya, Robert, I'll look after you. Won't I?'

Úna grins at her mother while Robert flushes.

'Now, Úna, there's no need for –'.

'– What, Ma, what?'

Joe enters the back porch, a stocky man with wisps of red hair in a thin comb-over on his shiny head. He removes his old raincoat and wellies and in purple fleck woolly socks he pads to the table. He walks with a slight limp.

'Hey, cool socks, Da. I'll have to borrow them sometime'.

Joe nods and sits in. Marguerite places a steaming dish with two rashers, four sausages and two eggs before him.

'Robert, would you like a fry-up?' Marguerite asks.

'No thanks, Mrs Toale'.

'He'll just have cereal'. Úna stands and stretches her arms upwards into a big yawn. 'It's okay, Ma, I'll do it'.

Both men avert their eyes as her t-shirt rides to the top of her tanned thighs.

'Yes, indeed'. She smiles at the tops of the mens' heads. 'I must say I had a lovely sleep'.

Marguerite sips her mug of tea, leaning her backside against the cooker, watching. Úna looks over at her mother.

'What?'

Marguerite keeps staring at her, an inscrutable look on her face.

'What is it, Ma? Does it not make you happy to see the fine body the Lord gave me? Hm?' Úna grabs a breast in one hand and a buttock in the other. 'It's the answer to your prayers surely. God knows you spend enough time –'

'– Within these four walls, the Lord knows what –'

'– I have to put up with. Yeah, yeah, Miss Melodrama 2011. But sure with hell on earth, haven't you all eternity to look forward to when you die'.

'Right, Úna'. Joe says.

'Okay, Da'.

'That's enough now. Get your friend his breakfast and move on'.

'Whatever you say'.

Úna turns to the cupboard and bends from the waist with her knees locked straight so that the full contours of her bum face the table when she reaches in for a bowl. The two men look away again. Robert stands.

'It's okay, Mrs Toale. I have to go. But thanks, anyway'.

Úna follows him to the back door and tries to kiss him but he dodges her. She returns to the kitchen and pours tea. The fingers of her hands wrap around her red mug and she sits in silence, a tiger that has lost its quarry.

Marguerite is wearing a flowery dress, her navy blue apron protecting it. She is polishing cutlery to go with her best delph stacked on the counter top. Her hair has been teased into tight curls and the dark roots are gone. She has on her strong perfume, the one she only wears on special occasions. There's a smudge of flour on her nose and her cheeks are red with excitement, like a teething baby. The kitchen table has trays of home-baked sausage-rolls, vol-au-vents, queen cakes, a coffee cake and a chocolate cake with a bowl of whipped cream covered in cling film in the centre. Each of the cakes have been cut into slices with a cake slice under one portion. The smell of sausage rolls fills the house. Every surface in the kitchen is gleaming.

A knock sounds on the backdoor and Robert walks in, one hand pulling at his fringe, the other holding his motorbike helmet. He's wearing his black leather jacket, a black shirt and tie and black trousers.

'Robert, come in. You look nice. She's upstairs. Go on ahead up'.

'Thanks, Mrs Toale'.

Úna is lying on her bed wearing jeans and a t-shirt, listening to her iPod. She wraps her index finger around and around a lock of loose hair. Posters of Limp Bizkit and Amy Winehouse look down on her from the sloped attic ceiling. She opens one velux window and looks out; the roof obscures the view of her home and garden. Perfect. That's how her life will be when she can leave this dump. She watches a bird alight from a branch. The branch swings backwards, like the counter movement of a rifle on the shoulder after the bullet's release. She smells the silage from the neighbouring farm and closes the window just as drops of rain on the wind touch her lips. Robert knocks and enters.

'Hello, dream boy'.

She holds out one arm as though displaying her bed.

'Take the weight off your feet, as they say'.

Robert kisses her with a light brush on the lips and lies down. He pulls sheets of folded art paper from his inside jacket pocket.

'Here. I got these back'.

Úna is putting on black eyeliner at the mirror.

'What ?'

'Your results for that art assignment'.

'Oh, that'.

'What?'

'He's a wanker'.

'He thinks your work is really good'.

'I wouldn't take any notice'.

'Why would he lie?'

'Why does anyone lie?

'I don't get you'.

'To get what they want'.

'He's not like that'.

'Yeah?'

'He's married'.

'He's married?'

'Jesus, Úna, that's really pushing it'.

'Right'.

'Well, I think you're dead wrong'.

Úna takes the papers from him and throws them in the bin. She pouts her lips to apply a dark red lipstick, painting the edges carefully with a black pencil. Then she opens her wardrobe and a mound of clothes rolls out. She rummages through, pulls out a short black skirt, then heaves the clothes ball back inside and leans on the wardrobe door to force it closed. She undresses and puts on a body-hugging, low-cut black top, a short skirt, fishnet tights and green Doc Martins. Robert watches her in silence. She turns to him.

'Well, Romeo, would you like me to paint some likkle black tears on your likkle sad cheeks?'

He continues to watch her.

She straightens up and looks at herself in the mirror from the front and the back, standing on a chair to see her legs.

'I'll do. Now, just my hair'.

She sits on the floor facing the mirror with her back to the bed. She starts to brush her hair. Robert sits up on the bed and places one foot on each side of her and takes the brush from her hand. Their eyes meet in the mirror. Slowly he brushes her hair while looking at her face. She looks down. When he has freed all the tangles, she closes her eyes and starts a French plait holding a green go-go between her teeth. He continues to watch her face, his hands resting on her shoulders. The frown leaves her face once her eyes close.

'Never could do these damn things with my eyes open. I lose my way'. She speaks muffled through the go-go. 'Like mirror writing; I can only do it when my other hand is writing in the other direction'.

He pulls her shoulders back so her upper back rests against his thighs. She relaxes into him as her fingers continue to work down the plait, adding hair from the side at each crossover.

'Thanks for coming tonight'. She says. 'It'll be dreary but she'd have a fit if I didn't show. Did you leave the fuckmachine out the back?'

'Behind the shed'.

'Good. It lowers the tone, don't you know. Her cronies from the church would not be impressed'.

She opens her eyes, ties the end of the plait with the go-go and turns around to face him.

''Good to have it all the same. Never know when you might need a quick exit'. She slaps his thighs. 'Showtime'.

'Ouch'. Marguerite smacks Úna's hand off a sausage-roll. 'Jesus, you don't have to be so mean, Ma'.

'They're not for you, Úna. They're for after the mass'.

'They're for me after the mass so?'

'Well, yes. Well, no, don't scoff them. Let the other visitors have them'.

'The other visitors. I'm a visitor now?'

'Ah, Úna, you know what I mean'.

'I see where I stand'.

'Would you leave me be'.

'Nice frock, Ma'.

Marguerite looks at her, not sure whether she means it. The doorbell rings and Marguerite rips off her apron and rushes to answer it.

'Father McIntyre, come in, come in. Let me take that and I'll show you the room. I hope it's okay'.

The priest is a small round man with red-rimmed eyes and a drinker's nose. He follows her into the sitting room where he arranges the table as an altar. Marguerite rushes around the kitchen readying a tray to bring into him. He walks into the kitchen.

'Oh, Father, I didn't think you'd come in here. This place is ... sure, now that you're here, take a seat'.

'– Sure isn't the kitchen the heart of any home, the engine room, where all the living is done'. He sits at the table beside Úna and Robert who are pilfering sausage-rolls.

'Will you have tea, Father, or would you like a small drop?'

'I never touch the stuff. Tea'll be grand'. He addresses Úna's breasts.

'You haven't met my daughter, Úna and her friend Robert. You know Robert is one of the Cummins's who own the petrol station'.

Úna turns around to Robert theatrically raising her eyebrows and grinning her approval.

'Well, it's a pleasure to meet your lovely daughter and Robert too'.

He shakes hands with them, gloving each of their hands in turn within both of his warm fleshy palms. Úna reflexly wipes her hands on her thighs after.

'Now Ma, see, even the priest thinks I'm lovely'.

'Now Úna', Marguerite forces a smile, but can't stretch it beyond her mouth so it looks more like a snarl, 'Would you stop that aul blather'. She turns to the priest, 'She's always pulling our leg, is our Úna. We can't keep up with her at all'.

The priest looks back at Úna's breasts. Úna smiles sweetly at him. The doorbell rings again.

'I'll get it, Ma'.

Úna stands. With her eyes on the priest, she pulls down her skirt and strides to the front door. Her face blanches when she opens it and she steps backwards.

'Úna? It must be'.

On the doorstep is a tall man with a wall eye in an army uniform.

'It's me. Don't you remember? Shane?'

A little girl stands beside him, her dódí in her mouth and her hand gripping his little finger. He turns towards the driveway, where a woman approaches with a baby. Úna backs away from the door and runs up to her room as Marguerite emerges from the kitchen to bring the visitors inside.

The house fills with neighbours and relations. People take their seats in the sitting room. Úna and Robert slip into their seats close to the door with the last of the stragglers. At the sign of peace, Úna shakes Robert's hand and gives him a tight smile. She smiles at Mrs O'Leary, a kind old lady from the village, as she shakes her hand with its dry papery skin. Her eyes find Shane, his wife and two children. So there he sits. Bold as brass. Pillar of society. His wife is beautiful; brown eyes, glossy blue-black hair and sallow skin. She's taken up with the baby who's sucking on a bunch of car keys. His daughter is sitting on his knee. His hand on her bare thigh. The long black hairs of his fingers, the wide tips of his square nails. The cuticle covering the lunula. The child swings backwards to look up at her father's face. He whispers 'boo' to her. Then she swings to the other side and he repeats the 'boo'. The honeymoon period.

The mass is over. Úna enters the kitchen where her mother is waiting on two kettles to boil to fill waiting teapots.

'What's he doing here?'

'Who? What?'

'You heard me'.

'Úna, I don't have time for this now. Be a good girl and bring in that tray, will you?'

'Would you stop pretending to be so fucking clueless?'

Úna starts crying and sits at the table hugging her knees. Marguerite goes to the window, placing both clenched fists on the counter and leaning her weight into them, hunching her shoulders. She looks out at the autumn leaves blowing up the windscreen of the family car. In a low voice she says.

'Life goes on'.

'Does it?' Úna's face streams with tears.

'What can I do?'

'Does it really, Ma?'

'What could I do then or now?'

'I don't think so'.

'What would you have me do, Úna?'

'It doesn't go on'.

'What?'

'It stays there'.

'Break up my sister's family?'

'Right in the place where it was left'.

Marguerite's voice rises as she turns to face her.

'Break up his new family?'

'Never budged'.

'Will that make it right? '

'Doing nothing didn't make it right'.

'Will that fix it?'

Úna's tears stop. She speaks in a monotone.

'Nothing. Nothing'll fix it.

'With us all in pieces?'

'You could do nothing, Ma. Nothing'.

Úna puts her feet on the floor, facing away from her mother. She sits with her back straight, her knees squeezed together, her palms pressed on her thighs, the toes and heels of her boots touching. Every part of her body clutching every other part to her.

Marguerite busies herself filling teapots. A blotchy red rash has spread up her neck.

'I had to invite family to the stations'. She continues. 'That's what the stations are about'.

'So what does that make me?'

'A blessing in your house surrounded by your family and your neighbours, your community'.

'Am I not your family?'

Marguerite has a blank look as though addressing a ghost in the distance.

'Of course you're my ...'

'Am I? Are you sure?'

'But my sisters and brothers, they are my family too. And their children'.

'No matter what?'

'No matter what'.

'And what about his little girl?'

'Ah, now you're trying to catch me'.

'Is she your family too?'

'Always trying to trip me up'.

'What about her?'

'Ah, he wouldn't do anything –'

'– He wouldn't?'

'He couldn't'.

'He couldn't'.

'Not his own flesh and blood'.

Úna stares at her mother.

'That's enough of that talk now. I have to serve these people tea. They must be parched with the thirst. What must they think? Úna, you start with this pot and I'll follow you in'.

Úna rubs her nose with her sleeve, stands and carries a pot of tea into the sitting room with a cup and saucer. She pauses inside the door to find him. She approaches Shane before she loses her nerve. As she gets nearer she decides to concentrate on a point between his eyebrows and not look into his eyes. That way he'll think she's not afraid. She finds a big brassy voice to use that's not hers.

'You'll have to introduce me to your little girl'.

She hands him the cup and saucer. Shane looks nervous. Same smell. Brute. You'd think he'd learn some fucking taste in all the intervening years. Jesus.

'This is Alicia'. He says. 'She is three. Say hello to my cousin Úna, Alicia'.

Alicia looks at Úna wide-eyed like she is an exotic animal. Her eyes zone in on her nose stud, her black varnished finger nails, her thumb rings, and her multi-coloured Doc Martin laces. She lets Úna take her small soft hand in hers. Her knuckles are dimples. Úna softens her voice for the child.

'Alicia, do you like dollies?

Alicia nods fervently.

'Then why don't you come with me 'cos I want to show you something you'll love'. Shane's face flushes and he turns to his wife. Úna starts to lead the child away, looking back over her shoulder to Shane's wife.

'She's just gorgeous. I'll only be a minute'. Shane's wife smiles at her and waves at Alicia. 'I just want her to see my dollies upstairs'.

When she reaches the other side of the room she sets the teapot down on the mantelpiece overhead and sits Alicia on her knee as she takes her seat beside Robert. Úna smiles over at Shane as she rubs the child's back, curling a stray strand of her blonde hair behind her ear. Robert plays 'round and round the garden' and 'this little piggy' with Alicia, through her open-toed sandals.

'Robert, will you take Alicia upstairs to see all the lovely Barbies? They're in the box on top of my wardrobe'.

Robert and Alicia leave the room, hand in hand. Shane stands up and Úna walks over to him with the teapot.

'Relax. Relax'.

'I don't –'

'– She's fine. Robert's great with kids. He's great really'.

Shane's face is white, his wall eye saccading the room.

'I'd rather she'd –'

'We're all family here. She'll be fine. Now what we all need after that mass is a good cup of tea. Sit down, Shane, and hold up your cup'.

Úna passes him a cup and saucer. With both of their hands shaking she starts to pour tea then stops. Her voice is older than it should be, even allowing for the stranger's voice she found inside her, but she can't stop it now that it has broken its bindings.

'Did you ever see the mad-hatter in Alice in Wonderland? I've always wanted to pour tea like that'. Shane's mouth is moving but she can't hear him. 'You were always game for a bit of craic, Shane. Hold it steady now'. She goes into falsetto. 'Steady'.

Shane's hand shakes more as he grips his saucer tighter. Úna lifts the teapot high and pours with a flowing up and down movement, like the body of a bird in flight that lowers as the wings rise. This takes the shake out of her hand.

'There. That wasn't so bad was it?'

She turns away before he can answer and pours tea for her neighbours then slips away.

Upstairs Robert and Alicia are sitting on the bedroom floor surrounded by naked Barbies and their tiny clothes. Alicia has a Barbie dressed in black but can't decide on the shoes. Robert offers a pair of sandals, not unlike Alicia's.

'How about these ones?'

'S'bwoke, wobut, s'bwoke'.

'What's broke?'

'The foots. Look. Pointy. S'bwoke'.

'She means the foot is broken because it is stuck with pointed toes'. Úna joins in, 'Fixed to wear high heels for life. What kind of shoes do you want for her, Alicia?'

'Them ones'. She points at Úna's green Docs. 'I like them ones. They's lovely and sparkly'.

Úna picks the child up so she straddles her waist. She looks down into the light of her face. To feel the openness of her soft little body, the absolute trust.

'I'm afraid Alicia, that Barbie has a disease in her feet and she'll never wear nice boots like mine. Now, time to get you back to your Ma'.

'Mammy' the child shouts with glee, suddenly remembering.

'And some sausage rolls'. Says Úna nodding at Robert.

'Sausagewolls' shouts Alicia even louder.

'Come on, Wobut', says Úna, 'I'm famished. Time for those sausagewolls'.

The three clump down the stairs together.

Notions

Concepta slides the gearstick of the black *Audi* into third gear and pulls out onto the dual carriageway leaving the city. On each side electric pylons rise up in the night, like masts of galleon ships. She straightens the crease of her pleated skirt and her dainty foot presses the accelerator to the floor. Leaning towards the rear-view mirror, she checks her hair. It falls in two blond curtains on each side of her slim face, the ends in straight lines. She's relieved to be on the road, away from the workload at home. Her husband can take over from the sitter at 6 o'clock and finish Jack's homework with him. She has left a casserole in the oven warming for the evening.

Concepta's car stops at temporary traffic lights in the country. There are no cars ahead or behind. In the dark she feels the shadows of the mountains close in on each side. She cuts the lights and the engine. She can see a shed on the brow of Knockmore. The stone wall of the field makes up one wall of the shed so the shed door opens directly onto the field. The economy of it. Why spare the stones for the wall of the shed, she wonders, when there is no shortage of stones in this rocky landscape? She hears the bog water running beneath the road. With a shiver she starts the engine again. She picks up the O'Brien/Higgins file. It is hard to believe these questionnaires were completed by two people sharing the same house, the same life together. She examines her red polished nails and returns the document to her bag. The traffic lights change and she drives on.

Harry O'Brien pulls up his collar and takes a drag from his cigarette in the smoking hut at Nortel. He is tall and wiry with a protuberant blue eyes. He was hoping to eavesdrop on Macken, his senior manager, but Macken has just left. Rain blows sideways into the hut and a few stray droplets land on the tips of his polished black shoes. He takes one more drag, exhales two flutes of smoke through his nose, then throws his cigarette in a puddle – tsss – and returns inside. He rests his weight on the edge of Ambrose's desk. Harry and Ambrose used to share packets of chocolate digestives at night in boarding school while discussing how far a boy could go with a girl and get away with it. These discussions have remained academic for Ambrose. He has a large head and an asymmetrical face, closer in shape to a parallelogram than an ovoid. He has always looked middle-aged even as a teenager and he speaks in a priestly way, a hangover from their schooldays with the Christian Brothers.

'How are you goin' on?' Ambrose says.

'Are you on for a quick one in the Trapper's?'

Ambrose pushes his chair back from the computer and stretches. He scratches the shaving rash on his double chin.

'Aren't you were meeting with yer wan in Ennis today?'

'They can wait. Bad cess to them'.

Tess Higgins sits back in her chair and surveys her staff through the glass walls. She doesn't know herself. Harry doesn't know her either any more or so he says. She has worked so hard to earn this. Mark pops his head in the door and she smiles.

'I should have the end of year medicines costing for you in the morning'. He says.

'Going surfing this weekend?'

'Hopefully. How are things at home?'

'I'm off now to another session. Torture'.

'Still staying with Mags?'

'Just on the days I'm not minding Davey. Once one of us'll move out, then Davey'll do the moving each week instead'.

'Not easy. Mind yourself'.

Tess puts her briefcase in her lap. She recalls slicing a cooked potato last night; it fell apart as soon as she touched it with the knife, as though the internal architecture was already broken. She pushes back her chair and puts on her coat. Tess has the statuesque gravitas of a heavy woman. She moves her bulk lightly on her feet like a ship, the thin fabric of her loose clothes trailing in flutters in her wake.

Concepta drains her second cup and holding it with her thumb and index finger, she replaces it in its saucer.

'Is he usually this late? We've a lot to cover, you know'.

Tess shrugs and looks at the floor, her fists pushing deeper into her coat pockets. They are seated in a windowless room, a partitioned section of the hotel conference room. They can hear a waiter moving delph on the other side of the partition. On a flip chart is a list of handwritten headings; Weekly Schedule with Davey, Parent-Teacher Meetings, Holidays, Passports, Wills, Family Home and Contents, Other Assets, Bank Accounts.

Harry walks in, his face flushed, his eyes glassy. He gives Tess a look, nods at Concepta and scans the room.

'God, this is some fuckin' dump. How much are they charging us for it anyway?'

'You're late'. Concepta says.

'Well, I'm not sitting in this kip spilling out my private business while some gobshite on the other side of the partition clatters plates and listens in'. Harry leaves.

'Just one minute! Hey …'

Concepta looks at Tess with a mixture of outrage and disbelief. Tess raises her eyebrows momentarily and retracts into her seat. Harry returns with the manager who apologises and moves them to another room. When they are seated again Concepta begins.

'I expect an apology, Harry, and an assurance it won't happen again'.

Harry holds out both hands palms up, like Jesus,

'Couldn't be helped. Mad busy at work. It's got to be done. Sure amn't I here, amn't I? Let's get on with it so'.

Concepta stares at him and glances over at Tess who looks out the window. Then for the first time Tess looks directly back at Concepta, her eyes undressed then she turns away again.

'Well, I've read through the questionnaires you filled in'. Concepta begins with a shake in her voice. 'And I have a better understanding of each of your points of view so I propose the following arrangements'.

Concepta stands and writes out a weekly plan, her marker squeaking on the cream page of the flipchart, her sheets of hair shaking with each movement. Tess feels Harry's eyes on her and glances across. He's staring at her feet. She pulls her coat forwards to cover her ankles. Then she looks back at the flipchart, though now she can feel him staring at her face. She wishes she had a carapace that she could retract her head and limbs inside, like a turtle. Concepta turns to face them.

'So, do you think this arrangement for Davey will work, Tess?'

'We can try it, sure, and see how it goes'. Tess replies in a small voice.

'Harry, how about you?'

He looks from Tess to Concepta and absently nods his agreement. His stare returns to Tess's face.

'So, I'm glad that's agreed. Now parent-teacher meetings;' Concepta continues in a singsong voice as if advertising *Readybrek*. 'Do you both normally attend?'

'Usually I go by myself'. Tess says.

'That's a lie. I went with you last year to that evening meeting. You're twisting things'.

'That was about the communion. Both parents had to be there'. She turns her body back to face Concepta. 'The parent-teacher meeting usually happens after school at 2.30. He can go if he wants to. Any time I told him about it before he said he couldn't get off work, that it didn't concern him'.

'From now on I'll be at every meeting connected with my son'.

'Fine'.

'Fine'. Concepta echoes in a mollifying tone, 'Then that's agreed. Now what usually happens with school holidays?'

'Well, I usually take a month's unpaid leave along with my month's holidays'.

Harry jumps to his feet, red-faced, shouting.

'God, you're painting yourself as a right martyr today, aren't you? Do you mop the kitchen floor with your hair too? Or maybe you starve so your son can have food on the table, though there's not much sign of that with the size of you'. Harry's face has a demonic look, his eyebrows furrowed down over his nose and raised at the edges like a cartoon character. 'The son you love so much you're going to break up his home, break up his family'.

'Harry, please!' says Concepta.

'You know what I put all this down to? Do you? Your work. It was a sad day for us when they promoted you. Before that you were happy. Happy with your life. Happy with me. But, then, then you got notions. Nothing was good enough for you, no. I'm not good enough for you. No one will be good enough for you'.

'Happy is it? Happy? No. Not happy. Bullied and trapped. Making the best of it. But you're right about one thing. Now I've a choice. Before I had none'.

Concepta cuts in.

'Harry, what do you think will work best for Davey for the holiday arrangements?'

Harry pulls his body back into his chair and looks at Concepta as if he has no idea who she is or what she is talking about. Concepta repeats the question and he replies in a muted tone,

'Fifty-fifty. Fair is fair. I want half of the holidays. Down the middle'.

Tess turns to Harry,

'But then Davey will miss seeing me. He's used to spending a lot of time with me. This is not a cake we are dividing, he's not an asset. He's a boy, our son'.

'Well, he'll just have to get used to it then, won't he? I don't want this anymore than he does. But I've no choice, have I?'

'But when you have him you don't spend time with him. You leave him with your mother'.

'I suppose you have a problem with her now, have you? Jesus, no pleasing you!'

'I don't believe this. You only want to see more of him to take him away from me. Jesus, it never occurred to me you would use him as a weapon'.

'This is all your doing, woman. I don't see you putting Davey's needs ahead of your own. We have you to thank for all this trouble. You're bringing this down on all of us'.

Tess turns to face Concepta again.

'I think Tess's point is important, Harry'. Says Concepta. 'If Davey is with you then it should be so that you can spend time with him. It's not something that you can delegate out to your female relatives. If that's what time with you means then Tess is right to push for more contact time with Davey if she will be spending that quality time with him. I think we should revisit this at our next meeting and you can both think about what is best for Davey in the meantime'.

Concepta works down the list to passports. Tess offers to apply for a separate passport for Davey and Harry agrees to sign the forms. Both agree to draft wills and to name the other as beneficiary of the life policy in case either should die prematurely.

'Well', Concepta beams, 'I'm glad all that is agreed. We're doing very well here. Now let's move on to the family home'. Harry sits upright, shouting,

'I'm not fucking moving. It's my house. I don't care what her problem is'.

Concepta coughs and straightens the pleats of her skirt. Tess looks inanimate and lumpen, the only evidence of life her shallow breathing and her eyes blinking, unseeing.

'Well', Concepta begins, 'as you are a married couple, by law the house does not belong to you Harry but to both of you. I know this is very difficult but agreement will have to be reached on this either by mutual agreement, or in court where it will cost you both, and it may still go against your wishes'.

'I don't like the smell of this. You two bitches have been plotting something, haven't you? Well, I'm not having it. I don't want this. I am agreeing to nothing and I'll sign nothing'.

He turns to Tess who stares at the ground in front of her shoes.

'You'll rue the day. You'll rue the day you ever crossed me. You'll never get the house. You'll never get Davey. You'll suffer for what you're doing, breaking up this family and all I did for you. I'll take you to the highest court in the land. You'll get nothing'.

Tess turns her whole body around to face him.

'I want nothing but to be free of you'. She says. 'I have never loved anyone as much as I have loved you. I have never been hurt by anyone as much as you have hurt me. You and your twisted love'.

She brings her right hand up to her forehead and with her palm facing inwards, she slowly draws it down like a blind as far as her chest, saying quietly,

'You are dead to me'.

Anger slips from Harry's face and his expression crumples.

'You can forget it, all of it. I'll agree nothing and I'll sign nothing!'

He knocks over the flipchart and flees from the room.

Concepta lifts and dismantles the flipchart, returning the files to her bag. Tess walks to the window.

'I thought this was supposed to be safe'. She says.

'It's a very difficult process for everyone involved'. Concepta's mouth smiles while a frown deepens on her forehead.

Tess turns to face Concepta.

'I trusted you'.

'But Tess –'

'– He's had more opportunity to attack me tonight than he ever had in the marriage –'

'Now, look –'

'– The difference is he now plays to an audience. You'.

'I know this must be very upsetting and stressful'.

'Upsetting and stressful, is it?'

'He's just too angry. He's not ready to be constructive. That's all this means'.

'Don't make excuses for him'.

'I'm not it's –'

'– It's not okay for him to plough roughshod through Davey to hurt me, whatever his reasons. I'm sick of him, searching the world for someone to blame, someone to hurt, when we are both losers'.

'But, Tess it's –'

'– Where would we be if I carried on like that? Why have I to be the grown-up? It's not okay'.

Tess reaches for her bag and trudges from the room, her arms hanging forwards of her rounded shoulders. The cushion of her seat slowly sucks in air to return to its original shape.

Concepta sits back in her chair, fully releasing her weight into it for the first time that evening. She feels a falling down in her bones. She looks out the window and watches Tess sit into her car. The hotel manager sticks his head in the door and looks around the room. He has the voice and haircut of a crooner.

'All done here, Concepta?'

'Just leaving, John'.

'Don't mind if I start setting up for the reception for tomorrow, do you?'

'Work away. Just waiting for the car park to empty'.

He motions to two waiters who bring in tables and cover them in sheets of starched white linen. They polish and stack champagne flutes in two tiers around a large silver bucket. John follows Concepta's stare out to the car park. Tess's car starts up and it crawls out of the hotel car park.

'Funny that, isn't it?'

'What?'

'All the fuss and bother over christenings, engagements, stags, hens, weddings and funerals. Everyone fighting to be part of it. Noisy celebrations lasting for days. Then a marriage ends'.

'A marriage ends?'

'And the world runs for cover while each member of the parting couple drags themselves through it, alone. '

'We're here, aren't we?'

'Can't be right'.

'A priest you should have been, John'.

'Couldn't give up the ladies. I'll stick with the pints and the room service. Will you be wanting this room again next week?

'Not likely'.

Concepta pays at reception and leaves. She drives along the dual carriageway and feels herself getting tired so she moves her car to the left margin where the interrupted white line beats against her tyres, helping to keep her awake. The rhythmic sound reminds her of a sewing machine, the road like material running through her tyres.

In the sitting room her husband lies sprawled on the couch asleep, Jack curled up in his pyjamas in his lap. She carries Jack to bed, his arms around her neck and his legs wrapped around her waist. She savours the clutch of his body onto hers and the little-boy-smell of his neck, a mixture of fabric softener and sweet sweat.

Idling

I'm outside their room. I can see the Ram's back through the crack in the door, tufts of black hair sprouting over that stinking vest. His breathing is regular. Good. I poke my finger into the jar of Vaseline and smather it all over the hinges. Reminds me of spreading Sudocrem on Ruby's bum when it's sore. I wipe my hands on my jeans and try pushing the door handle. Silence. Door opens no problem. The smell of booze, cigarettes and burning plastic chokes me but I don't cough.

His phone's in the back pocket of his jeans on the floor. I creep in, letting the heel of my foot down and transferring my weight through my foot before letting the other foot leave the ground. My Vans make no sound. I hate touching his stuff but I'm out of credit and this can't wait. He rolls onto his back and lets out a big snort. I freeze. My Ma lifts her head and looks at me with dead eyes, one breast bulging against the top of her nightie as though it'll pop out. Hate that. It's for him, of course. It's all for him. She says nothing when I grab his phone, just waves me out of the room and flops back.

I pull the front door of the flat shut behind me, turning the key so the lock slides gently into place, doesn't click. No one on the outside balcony, just Ruby's buggy. I lean my shoulder against the box-room window. Inside Ruby is grabbing her toes, laughing. She doesn't see me through the net curtain.

I write the last five numbers he's dialled on my hand, then I make my call.

'Hello, Mannion & Toomey?'

'Can I speak to Jacinta?'

'Just one moment, please. Who shall I say is calling?'

'Dylan'.

'Dylan. Dylan who?'

'Just Dylan. Look, she knows me. She said my case might be up this afternoon. I need to talk to her before she leaves for court. It's urgent'.

'Well, I'll ask her to ring you back on this number –'

'No. Here, I'll give you another number …'

Afterwards I dial his last five numbers, hanging up on each before they ring.

I go back inside, change and dress Ruby and sit her in her high chair. We're both mad for the Coco Pops. She's a smiler. That girl can say more with her face than any one I know with words. No need of them, she hasn't. Though that's not what they think down at the clinic. She has them baffled. The hearing is perfect. The development, as they call it, perfect – pointing at things, reacting, doing what she's asked. But not a word will she say for them. My little sister Ruby. Too smart for them.

When she's finished I clean the dribbles from her chin and toss her bib into the sink. I hear a rumble in the bedroom and then in comes Ma, an old cardigan thrown over her nightie, a fag hanging off her lip.

'Don't tell me ye finished all the bleedin' milk!'

'Damn all in it, Ma'.

'Jesus, Dylan, you know him, any excuse'.

'Okay, okay. Me and Ruby'll go down for it, won't we, Ruby?'

Ruby laughs and claps her hands in that way she has, the palms meeting and her pointy little fingers never touching.

'Get us some fags too while you're at it, son'.

She pulls a tenner out of her cardigan pocket and lays it on the table. I leave his phone down next to the tenner and lift Ruby.

'Come on, Ruby. People to see, jobs to be done'.

Ma looks up at me then at Ruby.

'Right', she says and pockets his phone and the tenner.

Hard to say when I noticed a change in her. Probably first time my Da was in jail, would have been before she met the Ram. Her family'd have nothing to do with her. She seemed to lose interest then, in everything, off her food, sleeping half the day, not bothered. Didn't visit him so often neither. But the worst was she stopped caring for Ruby. She'd look at myself and Ruby sometimes like she thought she recognized us but wasn't too sure, her own flesh and blood.

Da wasn't long out of jail when he got nabbed again. He couldn't face another spell inside, skipped bail. The white strip of skin on the back of his neck from his new haircut made him look weak as I watched him board the plane. Like a boy, not like a Da. Ruby's fleece smelt of his aftershave for ages after.

I'm carrying the buggy down the outside stairs when my own phone rings. Ruby's pulling at my ear.

'Stop, Ruby, not now'.

She thinks it's that game we play where I waggle one ear and she grabs it, crinkle my nose and she grabs it, stick out my tongue and she grabs it. Sharp little nails.

'That stuff was junk, Dylan!'

'They'll write that on your gravestone. "That stuff was junk Frankie Kennedy died on" – when are you planning on dying, Frankie?'

'You're in for it this time. You can't con him, you know'.

'Might be able to fit that on it too. Before the date and the year'.

'Laugh away, but he's not a happy man'.

'He's never happy, Frankie, never. So, what does he want now?'

'More hard drives, higher spec'.

'Can't have been too bad if he wants more'.

'You won't get that kind of money again, though'.

A pigeon flies down and starts pecking at the KFC wrapper in the bin next to the buggy. Ruby squeals and arches her back to be let out. She loves chasing them pigeons.

'What's that noise, Dylan? Where the fuck are you? Jesus, are y'at the slot machines or wha'?'

'I haven't seen the colour of his money yet. When's he going to pay me?'

'Don't you worry, you'll be paid. On the next delivery as usual. I'll be onto ye'.

The shop's closed, the shutters down, broken glass all over the ground. Opens at ten. I start pushing the buggy towards the 24-hour when the phone rings again.

'Dylan, it's Jacinta Toomey'.

'Howye'.

'I've gone over the file with the barrister'.

'Right'.

'It'll definitely be heard today'.

'I'll be in so. Who's on?'

'It's the new guy, Justice Gavin'.

'I'm fucked so'.

'Any chance your mother could come? That'd help, you know'.

I think of the day I walked in on them. The first day I clapped eyes on him. Her dimpled legs stretched wide and him on top of her, ramming himself into her and the terrified look on her face.

'Out!' he'd roared. Never even slowed. I grabbed Ruby off the floor of that room and legged it out of the flat. My Da wasn't gone two months at that stage.

'Dylan?' Jacinta was still waiting.

'No, not my mother, not a chance', says I.

'He could send you away. He could, you know, he's sent others down for less'.

I stare at Ruby. She thinks I'm joking again, doing my pretend-serious face.

'Dylan, are you there?'

'Yeah'.

'Well?'

'But I didn't hurt anyone. It was only a couple of laptops'.

'It was a government office, Dylan. Sensitive data. They take it personally'.

'But sure, I destroyed all the hard drives'.

'Even worse'.

'I can't go away. I can't. I'll do anything. Please'.

'Look, Dylan, you know how this –'

'But it's different this time –'

'It's the same crime as last time –'

'But Ruby, I've to mind my sister Ruby, she'll –'

'Are you her main carer then?'

'Yeah'.

'Okay, Dylan. Look, I'll talk to the barrister again and we might be able to do something with that. I'll see you at half three. Don't be late, okay?'

I start pushing the buggy up the hill to the petrol station. She's getting heavy, little pudding. At the turn I race down the smooth slope into the station and she jigs and shouts. Mad for speed she is, just like me.

Other lads love speeding and racing in robbed cars, for thrills like, leaving tyre marks in circles on the roads. Not me – too public, too much roaring and shouting, and too slow. Karting's my fix. Every time is like that first time. I go to the track alone, no one to distract me. I'm strapped in. My full-face helmet's on, pressing in on my cheekbones. My bum's just inches from the ground. I can hear my own breathing, in and out. It's like the whole kart is breathing, in and out. I push my driving boot to the floor and feel the vibration of the big doughnut wheels on the track. It travels up through my gloves, up my arms, rattling through my chest. The smell of the asphalt track mixed with burning tyres sears my lungs. I'm expanding, molten liquid to gas. The heat and the speed inflate me. I'm in the kart and I'm over the kart. I'm flying. I'm alone. It's the best place in the world.

I buy milk and fags for Ma, and a '99 for myself and Ruby. I take a few licks and pass it over. Looks gas, Ruby, the ice-cream nearly bigger than her head. She manages to eat most of it before it falls apart and we have to dump it.

It was Frankie's cousin, Charlie, that squealed. I never left any prints or nothing. He has the habit, Charlie. Gets into trouble and drags anyone he knows down too, to get himself a deal. Didn't take Frankie with him but.

I admitted nothing, of course. But they know it was me. Twenty laptops, no violence and not a lock broken? As good as signing my name. I've patience, you see. I can sit for an hour, two hours, watching the security man, waiting. When he nods off, I slip in and take what I need. Other fellas, they're a liability. Just want to talk. Or they want a smoke. Or they want to have a drink or ring their girlfriends or have the craic. They worry, they complain, they fidget. They get caught because they don't know how to wait. Don't know how to be still.

We stop at the playground. Ruby's a terror for the swings. If that swing could go over the top of the bar and down the other side she'd go with it. I push her for a while and along comes Karen with her young one.

'Howye, Dylan'.

'Howye'.

Her baby is only small so it doesn't go on the swings.

'Ruby's doing mighty. Won't know it now before she's starting school'.

'Whatcha call her? Your baby'.

'Lorraine'.

'Lorraine. Nice'.

Karen looks all different now. Before the baby, her eyes were painted black and her lips blood red and she'd never talk to the likes of me, let alone look at me. She looks younger now, no make-up, softer like. Gave up on that waster Jamie too. The baby'll always be his, though.

'Come on, Ruby. We'd better get you back to your Ma. See ya, Karen'.

'See ya'.

I'm standing outside the Four Courts waiting for Jacinta. Ma is minding Ruby. I go through security and into the building. Jacinta is talking to an old fella with a belly, a white wig and glasses. I give her the nod and go to the Round Hall. I ignore the nervous-looking fellas sitting on benches around the edges. I'm wearing my best Vans, hoodie and tracksuit.

I walk to the middle of the hall and raise my face to the light streaming in through the high windows. Then I close my eyes. I put on my helmet, my fireproof suit, pull down my goggles, climb in, click on my seatbelt and start her up. I can feel her purr right from the pads of my toes, up through my knees, my stomach, my chest, right up the back of my neck to the very front of my brain, behind my eyes. She's not moving but she's ready and willing. She's got a full tank in her, a new set a tyres and enough power to rise me and her off of this track when she wants to. But we'll stay here awhile idling and wait and see what it is we'll need to do.

If You Were a Boy

'If you were a boy, I'd go out with you', Katie says. She covers her mouth with her hand and giggles then slinks back to her gang.

'If I were a boy', Gwen whispers, 'I wouldn't waste my time with you'.

She sneaks looks after Katie for a few moments, then spins and lopes back to the classroom, wondering does it get any better.

Gwen is squat in build with thick eyebrows that almost meet in the middle and an unsettling stare. She has a sad mother and an annoying father. On balance the sadness is easier to bear. It makes no demands on her. Sadness naps in the afternoons and floats into space in the evenings. It is peaceful company, like having her black Labrador, Jett, on the rug beside her. Sadness loves deep breaths. It sighs. You can cuddle into it even if it doesn't respond. Everything is understood so no explanations are necessary. You don't have to pretend. You don't have to speak in code. You don't have to speak at all. Sadness never wonders how you are feeling and never doubts your words when you do speak.

Her father's jollity is like the nervous cheer at school when someone's mother has died. Neighbours and relations assure her how lucky she is that 'at least her father is well'. Well? For who?

Padraig O'Toole is a stud of a man, wasted on his plain wife. He works the markets at weekends selling jewelry so he is away from home two nights a week. To make up for this and for his wife's illness, he makes a special effort to be there for his daughter. She must be cheered up. She could go the way of her mother. Sometimes she regards him with the same flat stare.

His theory is that sleeping-in is the cause of mental illness so he doesn't stand for that in his house. Three alarm clocks ring at seven each morning. Both his wife and daughter know that his urgings and insistent singing, laughing and joking, 'It's a beautiful morning. You must get up now to see it. Come on. Come on. Up and out!' are soon followed by 'How can ye do this? What kind of madhouse is this? Get up. Get up. Jesus! All ye do is take, the two of ye. I can't stand it'.

If he gets to this point then all the energy of forced good cheer darkens to a simmering treacle. They are responsible for all his problems. They are his burden to endure. And most likely they will be the source of his difficulties in the future. Gwen enjoys these stories once she has heard them a few times. The details always change. She tries to guess whether it will be her fault or her mother's as to why he couldn't work in Amsterdam in the summer of '99. She realises – as her present enters the annals of his past – that there is little connection between events as they happen and the embellished versions of paternal martyrdom they become. This moves her out of his reach.

Gwen watches her mother closely. Sadness has different moods; sometimes it gets anxious, then the house is spring-cleaned. Everything goes to Vincent de Paul. Not just the old clothes she no longer wears, but the contents of her wardrobe and chest of drawers too. Then her father has to buy back all the family's clothes from the charity shop. Gwen and her father keep a stash of favourite clothes in two plastic bags hidden in the garden shed.

At other times sadness slows down. Her mother doesn't speak and her feet never leave the floor between footsteps. Food turns blue and green in the fridge and Gwen has to look after herself. But her favourite sadness is the giddy happy one; then her mother comes back to her in a double-dose of girlishness. She is chatty and twitchy, impatient to do everything at once, mad for action. She cooks three-course meals late at night. There's tandoori chicken made from scratch, banoffee pie, cupcakes with pink icing with sprinkles on top and tiramisu. There are haircuts, highlights, bikini waxing, fake tan, new makeup and clothes. It is both thrilling and exhausting. It usually ends with her mother overreacting to a saucepan of milk boiling over, or a ketchup stain on her shirt. Anger followed by regret, then the giddy energy evaporates.

On a mild September afternoon, Gwen walks along by the Corrib. In one hand she clutches a bag of *Tayto* while her other thumb rolls the flint of her cigarette lighter backwards to make a scratching sound. Jett bounds ahead and plunges chest-deep into the reeds chasing ducks. They reach a dip in the bank with shale and flat rocks at the water's edge. From there she is not visible to other walkers. Jett swims after the pieces of driftwood she casts into the flow for him. Then he weaves inland, nose to the ground. She lies into the hollow, pulling up her hood to cushion her head. She looks up at the sky. The clouds are tiered in cream stacked discs and there are bloblets left in a stream after a passing airplane. She eats her *Taytos* one by one. She remembers watching an empty *Tayto* bag perched at the edge of an open fire. Instead of flaming, it shriveled to a tiny version of itself, a miniature condensed *Tayto* bag, thicker and stronger with all the print still legible. When she finishes, she licks the salt from each finger and crumples the bag into her coat pocket. Then she sits up and calls Jett. His black head pops above the high grasses. She claps as he reaches her.

'Who's the loveliest, who's the best doggie woggie? Hmm?'

She strokes his face and presses her nose into his warm neck as she rubs him down. She returns to her perch on the rock and Jett settles down, his wet warmth pressing against the side of her leg. She pulls out a packet of *Silk Cut Purple* and bites off the plastic wrapper,

'See, smoking seriously damages your health. What do you think, Dr Jett?'

Jett looks up at her, tilting his head sideways.

'I know you'll never try this stupid habit'.

He sighs and lies down again. Junior Cert results tomorrow. She inhales and tries to blow smoke rings.

'So what'll it be? Am I clever enough to be a vet?'

The dog licks her free hand. She watches a tree stump in the flow of the river; the water rushes around it, sometimes lapping over the top of it. Long weeds are snagged and they flitter, turn and coil with the water rushing past. Watching the flow makes her think the tree is moving upstream. Like sitting in a train carriage when the carriage on the next track starts to move. But the tree is stationary. She stubs out her cigarette, returning the butt to the packet.

When she reaches the driveway, she holds her breath. The curtains are gone from the windows. The kitchen table is on the lawn, candles lit, set for two. The couch and chairs are lined up, the sitting room transposed to the garden. Her mother is standing in an upstairs window wearing Gwen's old school uniform. She reaches to the top small window cleaning it with a cloth, the pinafore riding up her thin mottled thigh. A middle-aged schoolgirl. Her father's van is gone.

Padraig slows his van as he approaches the toll bridge. Great to be on the open road. Long strings of misery, the two of them. Wasted effort. He glances behind him and smiles at his Harley glinting back at him. He spent last night shining her up. He straightens both arms and admires his bronzed hands gripping the steering wheel. He saw the boxercise instructor look him over last Monday night. And well she might.

'That's €1.80 please'.

'There you go, love'. he grins, 'Have a good one!'

It feels good to spread a bit of happiness about. God knows, his exuberant personality has been challenged. But he comes up trumps every time. It's all a matter of attitude. If you get enough sleep and exercise, look after yourself and work hard, the rest takes care of itself. Out of the side of his eye he sees two young lads working on a car engine. Would you look at the trousers plastered to them? Sculpted. And the swing of the hips. They'd have to be gay. Jesus. He presses his foot to the floor and feels his spirits rise. He'll set up his stall tonight, then a coastal drive on the Harley with Angela, her thighs squeezing him from behind, followed by a long boozy meal. She knows what a man wants, that's for sure. You have to take it where you find it. He lifts his mobile phone and turns it to silent.

Gwen sits on a stool in the kitchen eating beans on toast. Jett lies on the rug, his eyes following her mother's movements from room to room upstairs. Next to her plate the bean tin has stab holes in the lid and a sharp knife stuck in it. Her mother bursts into the room and looks around. She has sweat circles beneath both armpits. She takes the last two chairs, leaving Gwen sitting on the only remaining piece of furniture. Gwen puts down her plate and follows her mother out to the lawn. Her mother stands on the couch. Jump. Jump. Pause. Like a heartbeat. 'Adie' she whispers, 'Adie'. Her face looks like her holy communion photo.

Gwen spies Mary from next-door beckoning her to the hedge. Mary is in her fifties from the Islands. She is a rotund woman with language so heavily laced with curses they become endearments. She has the quirks of native Irish speakers used to the guttural liquid flow of their own language; the hard dental consonants of English slow up her speech so that every 's' is hissed or hished, every 't' brings a pause and even 'w's are slowed down with an added 'f' sound.

'Gwen, lovín. *Goile*. She's away with the fucking fairies again. Where's Daid?'

'He's gone on a trip. Can I try ringing him from your house?'

'Fucking men. Never there when you fucking need them. Come on in, *a stór*. Now, where's the fucking *fón*?'

Gwen tries her father's number. She sits in Mary's kitchen and watches the baby in the playpen. He's lying on his back pulling off the last binding of his nappy. He throws it in the air then grabs his penis, squealing with delight.

'The boys. They do love their willy. They do. Any luck?'

'No. I'll text him. He's sure to ring back'.

'He will, *a stór*. He will'.

They walk outside. Gwen's mother is sitting, bouncing gently on the springs. Squeak. Squeak. Pause.

'She's running out of steam. I'd better ring the Unit'.

'Do, *a stór*, do. It's for the best'.

In the kitchen, the baby is sucking the handset. He cries when it is taken from him.

'What's he called?'

'Yeara, they do call him some fucking weird name. I can't say it. Sounds awful like bastard. But we take no notice, do we?'

Mary picks him up, laying him flat in her broad aproned lap. She kisses his toes and pretends to eat them as he chuckles.

'Sure, that's no name for a fucking *garsunín,* is it? No name, at all. Muiris. That's what he answers to round here. There's a proper name and no 'ch' for the english speakers to fucking choke on. Muiris it is'.

She whistles the 'r' so the sound of his name runs from 'm' to 's' in one flowing sonorous syllable.

'Now, *a ghrá*. Back on with your vest and nappy 'cos *caithfeadsa dinnéar a chur sios. Sea, dinnéar domsa is duitse*'.

Muiris shouts.

'*Diní duití*'.

She straps his nappy on and returns him to the playpen handing him a digestive biscuit. Gwen returns the phone handset.

'They'll send Francie Greaney around. He'll have a look and see'.

'He's the usual fella, is he? He knows her way?'

'Francie's sound'.

Padraig lies sprawled naked across Angela's futon, smoking. The room is candlelit, perfumed with musk incense. Angela's chin rests on her arms. She watches his face. A blue light flashes from his phone on the table.

'Do you want to take that?'

She reaches across and hands him the phone. He frowns as he reads the text, turns the phone off and returns it to the table.

'What was it?'

'It's nothing. Just the usual stuff'.

He sits up and rolls a joint on an old Fleetwood Mac album while Angela runs the bath and shouts in,

'Don't forget to join me'.

From a chair in the hallway, Gwen watches her mother through the open door, waiting for Francie to come. Francie Greaney, a small man with broad feet and a springy step, waves at Gwen from the gate then sits himself opposite her mother. He has the staring eyes of a contact lens wearer, the whites visible above the iris. Her mother is stony-faced. She stares over his shoulder and gives few responses to his questions. Gwen brings out a navy woollen coat and wraps it around her. Her mother looks up into her eyes with a beseeching look then lets herself be led inside. Francie and Gwen move the furniture back into the house. Her mother sits wrapped in her coat and a blanket in the sitting room, her teeth chattering. In the kitchen, Francie leans against the counter, one hand in his armpit and the other holding a mug of tea.

'She got the bottle-sterilising equipment again'.

Gwen nods.

'Does she buy it every time?'

'She borrowed it from Mary. Dad can only give her a little money at a time, cos, you know…'

'She'll have to come in'.

'Sure, isn't she over it? I'm big now. Can't I mind her here?'

'You'll be at school. Last time she nearly …'

'I hate bringin' her in there'. Her eyes fill with tears and she pulls out her mobile to try her father again. 'All those fuckin' loonies'.

Jett presses his head between her knees. She spreads the flaps of his ears with the palms of her hands. They are like two warm boneless furry wings.

'Right', she wipes away her tears with her fingers, 'Let's go, so'.

Once her mother is settled, Gwen returns home. The house is dark and cold. She lights a fire and finishes returning the furniture and lamps to where they normally live. Then she makes a cup of instant coffee with hot milk and two slices of toast with butter and honey. She puts on a *Radiohead* CD, turns off the lights and lies down on the rug in front of the fire. She lays her head on the dog's chest and rubs his side. He shivers and whimpers in his sleep, and his back leg moves rhythmically scratching the air. Adie. She used to talk to him when she was small. She can't remember him now. Her mother can't forget him. Still the locket with his hair. Still his baby suits hidden in her old handbag at the back of the wardrobe. The only place Dad wouldn't find them. He'd hit the roof if he knew. As though getting rid of every piece of clothing would get rid of losing of him.

Gwen is at school early the next day for her results. She gets good grades in English, Maths, History and Science. The rest are just okay. At break time in the smoking hut Katie and her acolytes join her with two lads from the class, Jack and his shy friend, Carl.

'So, Gwendaloon', Katie grins back at her friends, 'coming to Millennium Madness later?'

Katie stands with one hand on her hip, the other tapping ash, pointing her index finger. She has brown eyes, a dental brace, thick lips and a curtain of straightened auburn hair down her back.

'Might be. Why?'

Katie puts a hand on Gwen's shoulder as she smiles back at her friends and whispers,

'Well, if y'are, Johnnie Rodgers wants to shift ya'.

Gwen pulls back.

'I'm serious! He does! Are y'on?'

Gwen doesn't answer.

'Well, are ya? Or maybe', looking back at her friends, 'you're a lesbo. Maybe that's it, is it?'

Her friends cover their mouths with their hands.

'I … I don't like you'.

Katie turns to her friends again.

'She doesn't like me, girls. I should be offended, shouldn't I? See ya later Gwendaloon. I'll text ya his number and you can show us which side you play on'.

They run off screaming. Gwen checks her texts. Her father has spoken to the hospital. He'll be back first thing on Saturday morning. She looks up. The boys in the hut throw down their cigarettes and stamp them out. Carl extends his arm in a ladies first gesture, then walks with Jack a couple of paces behind Gwen back to class .

On her way home from school, Gwen walks into the old graveyard and closes the stiff black gate behind her. Her fingers trail over the gravestones then she leans her back against the ivy-covered high wall. Funny thing about a weak spot. Soon as people know about it they use it against you. Can't resist. Almost as if they're jealous of it. You've got something they don't have so you must pay. Katie was her best friend until second class. Until that day they were playing upstairs and her mother burst in. Katie sat frozen through the full poisoning story, the carpets, the clothes softeners, the gases, the radiation, and even the timed electronic food bugs.

Gwen visits her mother. Orange short pile carpet covered in cigarette burns and squashed gum. The corridor smelling of pee. She brings her some carnations from the graveyard. They smell of cloves. Her mother is a zombie, constantly licking her lips, speech slurred, eyelids heavy. No harm. Means she doesn't have to see the madwoman in the next bed who picks invisible fluff from her clothes. Or the rocker in the hallway who repeatedly claps his hands, slaps his head and then the wall.

Gwen is cooking an omelette, wearing her best top and jeans, when the doorbell rings. It's Mary, with baby Muiris on her hip.

'Well, *a stór*, how's Mam?'

'Come in. I'm just cooking tea'.

'I won't stay. You've enough on you without me bothering you. This young buck will go mad'.

'She's okay'. Gwen turns the omelette and puts on the kettle. 'Safe, I suppose. Just zonked. It's an awful place'.

Mary looks around the kitchen then back at Gwen, looking her up and down.

''Tis a fucking awful place. Faith and it is. You're all dressed up, girl. Have you a dance on?'

'Millennium Madness. You know, Junior Cert'.

'Your results?'

'Well, I …'

'*A dhiabhaill*, girl. Show me. Show me. Hush, a Mhuiris'.

The baby tries to escape onto the floor. Mary holds him tight, squeezing his thigh with her thick fingers, the wedding ring embedded in her flesh. With her free hand she shakes the creases out of the page Gwen hands her.

'A ss and B ss. Aren't you the wonder? *Comhghairdeachas, a chailín*, is it a professor you'll be?'

Gwen smiles. Her even teeth a surprise. Her hazel eyes fill with light.

'A vet. That's what I want. To be a vet'.

'Then 'tis a fuckin' vet you'll be. No fuckin' doubt about it, *a chailín*'.

'*Diní*' says the baby, swinging backwards, reaching for the omelette.

'Yes, yes *a ghrá*. *Dinnéar* it is, but 'tis not yours. *Téanam*'.

She turns to Gwen as she leaves.

'Congratulations, Gwen, you're a fucking mighty girl, a mighty girl altogether! Be in no rush with them boys at the dance, girl. No rush, at all. Stick with the girls. Stick with your friends'.

Gwen is blow-drying her hair when she hears her father's van pull into the driveway. He calls her from the hallway.

'Coming' she shouts down, 'just a minute'.

He's sitting at the table drinking coffee.

'Hi Dad, I wasn't expecting you back until the morning'.

She's wearing jeans, platform shoes and a crop top. Her child's belly protrudes over the belt of her jeans.

'Signs on it'. He looks her up and down. 'What are you all dressed up for? Planning a party here or something?'

'God, Dad. It's Millennium Madness, you know'.

'Well, you're not going in that get-up'.

'What? This is new. It's my best top. I bought it with Mam'.

'I don't care if you bought it with the queen. You're not wearing that to a dance'.

'But, Dad? I like it. It suits me. Everyone's wearing them'.

'No daughter of mine is going to a dance half-naked. Go and change'.

'God, Dad, you're so old-fashioned'.

'Now', he shouts and slaps the table with his hand.

She clumps up the stairs and changes into a plain blouse and hoodie.

She is sitting in the passenger seat of the van as Padraig reverses out of the driveway.

'You don't have to drive me, you know'.

'I'm driving you and that's that'.

'I can go home with Katie and the girls'.

'I'm collecting you, too. Eleven o'clock on the corner. Be there'.

The van stops at the traffic lights and they sit in silence. A couple in the car ahead engages in a languorous kiss, mouthing each other's tongues and lips. It reminds Gwen of a video she played and reversed in slow motion of a dog giving birth, the slow covering and uncovering of the puppies with all that slime. The lights turn green. Padraig beeps his horn. The car ahead pulls off.

'Did you see her?' Gwen asks.

'Called in on my way back'.

'What did they say?'

'Couple of weeks, the usual'.

'Would you mind not, you know ...?'

'Would I mind not pulling my van up in front of all your friends? Terrible, isn't it?'

'It's not that. It's just ...'

'Forget about it. Hop out on this corner and I'll be here at eleven. Have fun'.

'Thanks, Dad. Sorry'.

'Yeah'.

Gwen gets out of the van and waves back at him then walks around the corner towards the queue of children behind the barricades. She joins Jack and Carl at the back of the queue. Up the front is Katie wearing a white crop top, a miniskirt and white heels. She looks cold beneath the fake tan. She screams each time one of her friends arrives; they kiss, hug and compare clothes.

'Omigod. Omigod. You look fantastic'.

'Oh, I love your shoes. Omigod, where did you get them?'

Carl turns around to Jack and does a silent mime of Katie's antics with air kissing, facial contortions and hand movements preening imaginary long hair. Gwen giggles. Katie sees this just as Johnnie Rodgers arrives. He is ambles along with the fluid movement of an athlete.

The doors open and the children crowd inside. Though they range between thirteen and fifteen years, they are a varied group. The smaller boys and girls are dressed conservatively in clothes of their parents' choosing. The older girls wear crotch-short miniskirts, thongs, stilettos, push-up bras, and tight tops with low-neck lines or crop tops, like bras worn as outerwear. The older boys wear hair gel, brand name T-shirts, oversized jeans or tracksuits and runners.

Once inside the dancehall, Gwen starts to move with the music and Colm, a boy who attends her horse riding classes, asks her to dance. He is shy. She is relieved to be away from the pack of girls at the wall. Once the music stops she makes her way to the mineral bar. Katie taps her on the shoulder.

'Didja get my text?'

'What? No. I –'

'– Didn't I tell ya, Johnnie wants ta shift ya. Nine o'clock at the front stairwell on the second floor. Don't be late'.

'Oh. Okay. But …'

'What?'

'But, what do you … do, like?'

'How diya mean? Shiftin', like? Ya mean ya don't know?'

Gwen shakes her head.

'Jesus, ya haven't a clue, have ya? He sticks his tongue in your mouth, like, and holds ya real close. But ya don't let him put his hands anywhere'.

'How do you mean?'

'Ya know, privates, like. That'd be disgustin', like'.

'Oh'.

Katie's friends pull her away and Gwen returns to the dance floor with another boy whose forehead reaches her chin. He dances a slow dance with his hips thrust forwards so she has to stick her bum backwards to avoid him.

At nine o'clock Gwen climbs the stairs to the second floor and walks along the dark corridor towards the front of the building. It smells of pencils, rubbers and old runners. She hears a panting sound ahead of her and the beat of the music behind her. Light beams across the hallway from the open door of the boys' toilets. She reaches the stairwell. Tied to the newell post is Smokey, an old stray black terrier with the school scarf tied around his neck. Gwen bends down to free him. Stifled giggles emerge from the balcony above.

'Hah, fooled ya!' Katie shouts down. 'Bet ya thought I was serious'.

She and her two friends come down the stairs sniggering. Gwen continues to untie the dog.

'Ah, come on. Ya didn't really think Johnnie Rodgers would be into you, did ya?'

Gwen strokes Smokey, keeping her eyes down. Under her breath she says,

'Fuck off'.

'What did you say?'

Gwen stands to her full height and slowly looks from Katie's face down to her feet and back up again.

'I said fuck off Katie Dillon. Stay the fuck away from me or I'll set my dog on you. And my name is Gwen. G-W-E-N. Got it?'

Katie flushes.

'Come on Katie'. Her friends pull her away. 'Leave it. Leave it. Joke's over. Let's go'.

Gwen watches as the three girls run off down the corridor. A puff of smoke billows out from the boy's toilets. She bends down again to open the last knot on Smokey. Then she straightens up and watches the dog trot down the stairs, his nails clicking on the marmoleum steps. Carl approaches from the boys' toilets.

'Hi Gwen, will you come for a dance?'

'Sure'.

Carl imitates a girl pulling down a short skirt. Gwen giggles then she imitates a boy combing gelled hair as though her fringe stands stiff over her forehead. They walk down the corridor towards the music.

Fracture Threshold

John lay still on the stretcher while a red tide of blood spread slowly up the white sheet from his groin.

'I'm safe'. He said. 'Thank God, it's over'.

A tall man with a caved-in look, John walked with out-turned feet. In recent times he had become a mild man, a man of few words. He had become what women describe as 'easy in himself'. He didn't get excited or disappointed about who won the football, he didn't seem to notice the children, whether they were in hysterical giggles or in inconsolable tears. He didn't appear to notice what his wife cooked for dinner each evening. After the meal he would say the very same thing.

'That did me nicely, I've had my enough for today'.

His wife, Anne, was a small woman with a quick temper, rosy cheeks and a husky voice. She was the kind of woman who would reach in front of you in a supermarket or stand too close in a queue even when you moved ahead to give her space. Once she had an old friend to stay.

'That man is so laid back', her friend joked. 'He'd eat the

same evening meal forever'.

Anne smiled, but the idea worried her. She decided to put it to the test. She cooked him spaghetti bolognaise every evening for two weeks; he didn't show that he had noticed. She changed the meal times, tried exotic recipes with strange tastes, such as chillies and pickled vegetables. For weeks she left out meat and fish; then all vegetables. He never wavered.

'God blast him'. She said. 'I'll get a reaction from him yet'.

She studied his movements and responses over time.

'It's worse than I had realized'. She thought.

Each day he got up before her, ate his breakfast alone slowly in silence, like a lodger. The sound of munching filled the kitchen, like a horse eating red apples. Then he smiled at each of them as they sat down to breakfast. He sipped his mug of tea as attentive as the family labrador, until it was time for the children to bundle into his car for school. He offered his cheek to her for a kiss, like collecting a ticket from a parking meter, then out the door until five.

'I'm married to a man who speaks three sentences each day. The same three. This can't go on'.

Other parts of his day had a predictable routine; he worked alone in the factory sterile room, testing stents used for heart surgery. From each batch of stents two were randomly selected. John's task was to place each of these in a device that would put them under increasing pressure until they fractured. He recorded the fracture threshold pressure and reported any substandard batch which was then destroyed. Each lunchtime he ate his 'any sandwich' as the children called it, at the window seat in the staff canteen. Each evening he read the paper, watched the news and fell asleep on the couch. He awoke when Anne turned off the television.

'So, it's time for bed'. He said. His third sentence.

Weekends, fishing by the canal or tinkering with his old Volkswagen replaced his workday routine but his three-sentence limit did not alter. Even during 'activities' as they playfully called sex during their early years, John was remote.

'I think there's something wrong with him. This is not the man I married. Until I know what's what, I am not going to touch him again'.

John gave no outward sign that he had noticed.

Their 8-year-old son spent hours rolling his tanks and missiles along the floor in silence while his father read the paper. Their younger daughter was content to play house with her imaginary friends in the Volkswagen on Saturday mornings while John worked on the engine. The children never spoke to him directly but about him instead.

'Is he home yet? Has he started the car? Is he still watching telly?'

'I wonder that they even need to ask' Anne thought. 'But if its silence he wants then I'll soon flush him out'.

But Anne was wrong. John was more alive than he had ever been. Each day he thought he would burst with the surges of joy he experienced. Vivid colours welled up within reach of his touch. Word sounds danced around the walls for hours after speech ended. His fingers could feel the texture of a surface from three inches away. No matter what he ate, all food tasted like pecan nut ice cream. All smells became the smell of browning croissants. He could see the colours of the threads that connect people. When no one was looking, he ran his finger along them and could hear the deep tones contained in each. He understood now the code hidden in the movement pattern of the branches in the wind. Pi extended to infinity and he knew how to map that movement pattern from a certain point along that number sequence; he knew what the next movements were and he stared for hours at the trees. It was like humming along to a tune you love.

The magic came to John one day six months before, when he was peeing into the river on his way home from fishing. The sky darkened then a mauve light came over the water. He felt a surge of power, an electric shock, travel up the arc of his urine into his penis and then spread like an orgasm through his body. Over the hours that followed he was overwhelmed by sensory experiences; a wealth of sights, the textures of colours, the visual dances of sounds along with a convergence of all the tastes and smells to his favorite two. Over the following weeks he adapted and learned how to enjoy these new sensations. The key was to experience no more than two senses simultaneously. He was most sensitive to sound. If he minimized his sensory input then his experiences were pleasant and they enriched his life. A top-up occurred once a week when he peed into the river on a Friday.

Anne started her campaign by joining him at times he was usually alone. She rose early to eat breakfast with him. He ignored her when she spoke. The following day he got up even earlier so she missed him.

'Look at me. Talk to me' she implored. He avoided eye contact and hurried to work.

She called to his workplace at lunchtime and sat across from him. Talking. Talking. He glanced at her periodically with the look of a trapped animal, and finally escaped her by going to the bathroom. She sat across from him in the evenings, pulling away his newspaper. Talking. Talking. Talking. He stormed out of the house.

For the next three weeks he avoided the river walk, all top-ups and physical contact. Yet the colour auras around people continued, sound shapes moved around him, his wife's unspoken words jumped from chair to chair and lodged in the seat cushions and later released when one of the children sat down. All smells had changed to silage and all tastes to fried kidneys.

He normally turned to Anne for 'activities' on Saturdays if he was interested. He had got away with going straight to sleep on the last two occasions. That Saturday evening he looked at the old ruin on the hillock behind their house and started walking towards it. As he walked, he watched a feathery long white cloud move across the sky in the shape of a skeletal giant. He passed a row of trees of different heights, all had lower leaf lines at the same level, like a woman lifting layers of her skirts so they don't touch the water.

While he was out, Anne sat at the kitchen table, drumming her pink fingernails on the varnished oak. Had he just turned away from her? Or was he turning his attention towards someone else? She pulled out the family accounts. No bills out of the ordinary in the bank account or credit cards. She checked his jacket and trouser pockets, turned out his sock and underwear drawers. No receipts apart from lunch and spare parts for the VW. It was Saturday night. It had been three weeks. It was time.

John got home late, wet through with mud spattered to the knees of his trousers. His eyes were glazed. He showered, ate his reheated evening meal of bacon, cauliflower, cheese sauce and potatoes, then tousled the children's sleeping heads.

Anne turned and lifted the covers for him. He lay on his back in his pajamas and closed his eyes.

She placed her hand on his stomach and traced two lines up to his nipples.

He felt numerous hands on his chest twirling and shaping, cupping and pulling so his skin felt rolled off his ribcage.

She raised her fingers and lightly trailed her fingertips over his stomach and groin, down his inner thighs.

He felt the tickle-itch of hundreds of soft dreadlocks sweeping over his trunk and upper legs. The movement was like the wave of a jellyfish as it wafts its friable edges in and out to propel forwards. The hands continued to mould his chest.

Anne rolled on top of him and guided him inside her.

He shuddered with the intensity of two women's' bodies driving and grinding their hips against his thighs, their tongues in his ears, their fingers in his mouth while two more hands tickled and teased his genitals and anus then –

– Anne rose onto her feet hunkering above him, raising and lowering her hips, she reached for his face forcing him to look at her –

– He felt a man's firm grip on his hips from beneath, then pressure, pressure – the noise of a braking train screeched in his ears, the sound of shattering glass showered the room with splinters. As he looked in her eyes large orange balls bounced through the walls then were sucked through the ceiling.

He broke away, rolling out of bed, brushing glass shards from his body. He staggered to the bathroom and locked the door. His pee was purple, a C note pulsing through it with an overtone of C an octave higher alongside. The notes dropped like balls of mercury onto the floor. He took the nail scissors out of the cupboard and started to cut. The colours and sounds seeped away with the pool of blood.

He unlocked the door smiling, finally able to look her in the eyes.

'Mother of God!'

'It's okay', he said. 'It's over'.

FLOCK MEMORY

Sometimes people act is if, live as if. They go through the motions as though nothing has happened. They get up in the morning, shower, eat breakfast then go to work or study. They speak to others, share a joke and even find a laugh from somewhere. The clue is in the delay in response time, the pause before reply. It is possible to be next door to feeling most of the time. It just requires effort.

She found herself sitting beside Tom at the first lecture. It was the initial candidness on both parts that attracted. He was closer to seven foot tall than six. He noticed the colour difference between her eyes, one green the other tinged with a hazel fleck. She saw his *séanus,* the gap between his two front teeth. Their conversation was of lecture schedules and choice of subjects. Then the rhythm slowed, as though to allow all their unexpressed thoughts pass between them. Thoughts that could not be netted by words. When they stood, her head reached his elbow. Marion lurched to the right, taking the weight off her clubfoot.

'God, we're some pair', she said, surprised when she realised she had spoken aloud.

'I won't ask about your foot if you don't ask about my height'. He replied.

'Deal', she said and that was the beginning.

Marion inserts her foolscap pages into her folder, clicks it shut and stares into space. When she feels him leave the lecture hall, she picks up her blue satchel and puts on her coat. It requires vigilance but mostly she manages to sit five or six rows away from him during lectures now. Any closer and her concentration is shot. Even if she can't hear him, she imagines she can feel him breathe or catch his sandalwood smell. She imagines touching the nape of his neck again or the dry silvery skin along his instep. She pictures the overshoot of his fingers, light passing through his nail beds, when they held their two palms opposed, prayer like, to the window. She remembers the hot stuffiness of lying together under a white sheet, forehead to forehead, making day night, whispering and rebreathing each others' breaths like one large animal.

Once he leaves the lecture room flanked by his two friends, she relaxes and slowly makes her way out in her antalgic rhythm. As usual, Olwyn asks her to join them for lunch. She declines. She walks into the bright windy day and on home. Clouds chase each other across the sky as though in fast-forward.

The household is consumed by her younger sister's melodrama. Her mother is taken up with setting right the endless chaos Fiona creates. Dympna O'Toole is never sure what really has taken place. She doesn't trust Fiona's account. Yet she doesn't believe her daughter is a liar. Her sister and three brothers are already seated at the table when Marion sits into her place.

'But I never hit him. I never did', Fiona insists.

'Let it go, Fiona. Let's talk about something else. Hello, Marion, how are you getting on?' Her mother asks, looking relieved.

There is no need for a response. Fiona curses at one of her brothers for imitating her and is thumped in reply, so Dympna O'Toole is drawn away again. Marion eats the lamb stew and a few carrots. She leaves the potatoes. Too many vegetables cloud her thinking.

After lunch, she slips away from the family table with a cup of tea. She locks her bedroom door and smokes a cigarette out the open window, looking across into McFadden's backyard. Their greyhound on a chain, circles the shed and whines to her, then lies down and continues to whine. Fingers Mc Fadden. The name should have been a giveaway. She sees now of course. Someone always knows. It's part of the flock memory. It's just no one spells it out. Would she have believed it if they had? Probably not. She stubs out her cigarette on the underside of the red brick window ledge and sees her footprints in the mud outside, visible still three months later. She hides the cigarette butt and closes the window.

Fingers is standing in the shade of the back door watching smoke curl from his neighbour's window. He flicks his cigarette butt into the mud and snorts. He is a wiry man with large hands and feet, short legs and greasy shoulder length hair. In his own mind his long locks are in the style of a famous soccer player. A cloth cap disguises his receding hairline. He sweeps his imaginary fringe back over his head, resting his hand on the back of his neck. His callused fingers, dirt ingrained in the creases and under the nails, are as thick as they are wide. They have that swollen look of one who normally works in the cold and whose fingers swell and throb indoors. He looks out over the yard at the long shadow of the bungalow thrown by the winter evening sun. The shape of the chimney overlies the boundary wall, a smoke shadow touching the top, like a child on tiptoe trying to reach for the ceiling. The smell of grilling mackerel reaches him. He turns back into the house as old Mrs McFadden calls him from her bed. He ladles the egg onto the fried potatoes, onions and mackerel and places it alongside a glass of milk on a paisley patterned tray. Then he stamps his way up the stairs, the grit on his tipped boots scritching each tile step.

Marion takes out her books and starts work on her maths assignment. Numbers are comforting; they follow rules. Even exceptions are clearly highlighted in advance so you couldn't mistake them for anything else. She notes down her answers neatly in green ink. Then she goes to the piano to practice her scales and the piece she has just started to learn. As she plays, her face loosens and loses all expression. Her right foot rises and falls to a slow rhythm, a rhythm different to the music played. When she stops she sits in silence staring at the music book. In the background are the sounds of her family; her mother's hushed tones on the phone to her aunt, her brothers regaling each other about the fistfight in the schoolyard that day and Fiona upstairs singing to herself in the bath, her one place of calm. She smells frying onions and garlic from the curry prepared in advance for dinner.

She remembers how once it was over the other girls crowded around her, asking questions about him and their time together, sniffing for blood. She was elusive. In exchange for sympathy they expected they had the right to feed on her story. She distanced herself. There was a safety and a purity in it. It was unadulterated by the taint of other people. That made it manageable. It also meant she had to place time limits on thinking about it. If she didn't then it would consume her, turn her into an adult version of Fiona.

Marion closes the piano lid and swivels off the seat. In the hallway, her mother puts down the phone as Marion puts on her coat

'Away again so soon, love?'

'Off to the homework club'.

'I don't know where the time goes'.

'It's okay, Mam, it'll be okay'.

She half-smiles as she rubs her mother's upper arm. Her mother stands in the doorway, arms akimbo, watching her leave.

Marion waits at the bus stop and plugs in her earphones. She leaves her iPod turned off as the earphones alone ward off approach. They muffle all extraneous sound. She dislikes overhearing conversations. People have so little to say that is worth hearing. They don't say what they mean. Maybe they can't. So much is unsayable. It is complicated living in this town. It isn't so small that you just say hello to everyone. That would be simple. Instead sometimes they say hello, sometimes they don't. Sometimes she misses a greeting she should have returned or someone fails to respond to hers. Earphones obviate the need to be present to anyone.

Her bus drops her at the Youth Centre. Sister Michael, a bubbly nun with a moustache and red cheeks, welcomes her.

'Marion, great. Just the girl we need. Over here, now. Jason, Caitlin, and Mike, take out your sums homework'.

Jason is nine, with a shaved head and the kind of freckles that stand out on pale skin. Caitlin is seven with long fair hair tied tightly back and frizzy tendrils surround her face in ringlets from the rain. She has hungry, searching eyes. Mike is a roundy-faced boy aged ten, who only really comes to the club to chat and have the craic. Marion has worked with them for the past two months. In the first session she had spent time explaining her clubfoot. Caitlin wanted to know is it all bloody, no, did someone stamp on it, no, does it still hurt, sometimes, and do people make fun of her, no, well, not to her face any more.

At five o'clock the sound of tights rubbing heralds Sister Michael's approach to call an end to the session and the children are collected. Then it's time for tea and biscuits for all the club helpers in the kitchen. It is amazing how little she actually has to speak; so many people talk for two. Sister Michael tells circuitous stories about herself and the difficult situations she gets into. Marion listens for the quirky habit she has of quoting herself; 'As I always say ...'

After the homework club, Marion refuses offers of lifts and takes the bus home. After dinner she returns to her room, locks the door and sits looking at herself in the mirror. Often she has conversations with herself in whispers. She relates both good things and bad, both thoughts and happenings. She says the things she cannot trust others with. Life feels real only when she has informed herself in this way. This evening she finds she has no words to unearth. She feels them queuing. They will come. Some days she can't abide looking into her own eyes.

She lies down on her bed, plugs in her iPod and switches to the one piece of music that brings her back into the fill of herself and inevitably to him again. Afterwards, empty and spent she whispers, 'Will he ever just go. I am sick to death of him'.

She takes out her anatomy textbook and starts learning the Latin names for all the coverings of the brain. When she has memorised these and the brain's internal chambers, she flicks to the section on the structure of the male organ. The majesty of its design; one-way valves that expand it to a tumescent probe. Then other images slide in of syphilitic chancres, penile discharges of yellow and green globules of pus. She smells it again. She feels sick in her stomach, winded. He must have seen her with Tom. It happened the third and last night she climbed out the bedroom window. She felt Finger's spade-sized hands grip her shoulders and swing her into the side shed. It happened so quick that she froze. She pictures his knuckles whitening with the grip. All knowing, all awareness, all being, sucked itself up from her fingertips, from the pads of her toes, up through the hollow of her legs, her arms. She stared up into the rafters to a gap between the roof tiles. All feeling funneled through her torso, her neck, out through her eyes, like a bunch of wires being pulled through a duct. It escaped through a gap in the roof, stringing in the branches of the horse chestnut tree overhead. She lay there for a long while after, waiting for herself to come back, willing herself to reinhabit her body again. Afterwards no amount of showers or baths could clear the smell even after a course of tablets from the doctor. She'd have to fillet herself to get rid of it.

She did not go to see Tom that night and made excuses for the rest of that week. She could not touch him for weeks. Some part of her had not come back, would not come back. She could see it in the mirror in her room but couldn't reach in to grasp hold of it. It was no surprise when Tom announced that he had been to the doctor, and was diagnosed with a sexually transmitted disease. He had a hard sad look in his eyes. She had no answer.

'Well, that's that then', he said.

'I suppose it is so', she replied.

But it wasn't really. Tom may have left her side but his body is within hers still. Her fingers can feel the firm dry skin of his back, the soft baby skin on the inside of his elbows. Her neck, his final shudder, exhalation and then his heaviness. Her thighs, the hard stretch-squeeze of wrapping around him, her feet interlocking his shins, so their bodies are completely stilled, all sensation focussed on gloving him to the hilt. Her chest, the deep reverberation of his voice through his spine, through her rib cage, as she holds him from behind. Her mouth savours the mushroom texture of him, his saltiness. Her stomach, moist with shared sweat, the coolness of the draft of air reaching it as they unpeel from the slick of each other.

She opens the window to smell the vegetation, turns off the light and from her bed looks out at the clear night sky. The night flight from Dublin circles the bay before turning in to land.

There is no disconnect. No switch. There is no release. Just a gradual washing away like the tide, where the silt of him gradually disperses out to sea. Meanwhile, she will act as if, live as if.

SEGUE

I knew we had an open marriage but I never expected to share a bed with his mistress. I first met Laurence on a wet windy Friday evening. I was clearing a window table in Maguire's Café when I saw a tall man in a navy Crombie coat wrestling with a yellow umbrella outside the door. In vain he turned the umbrella into the wind to try to force the upturned spokes to snap back down. It was like forcing a tight polo neck over the head of a resisting child. With a long loping step and a fop of brown hair falling over his high forehead, he took the window seat and sat staring out the steamy window, a copy of *The Heart is a Lonely Hunter* laid before him on the table.

I was in my final year in Business Studies. I had just had my heart broken. Mark had sparkly eyes, a stutter and charm that had melted me. I was slow to engage but once I started to love him, it grew and his interest waned inversely until finally he finished it. In the week prior to meeting Laurence, I promised myself each day I would not contact Mark again, though I ached for him.

Laurence had a beaten look, as though I was privy to his thoughts. He added one teaspoon of brown sugar to each cup of tea, tapping the teaspoon against the side of the cup before resting it again on the saucer. He came at the same time each day. After a week I asked him about the book.

'I haven't got to it yet', he replied.

After that I felt his eyes on me as I moved around the room. As though speaking with him had made me real. When he addressed me, he scanned my forehead, my eyes, my lips, then back to my eyes again, like a newborn baby might. Laurence's look was a searching one; into my person rather than over me as a woman. Within weeks we were spending much of our time together, melded by our broken parts.

Soon after I started an internship with Xerox Corporation. Sales techniques are to bullying what boxing is to violence. At last, tools to get what you want from people when they don't want to give it. I learned to use vulnerability as a weapon. Whining and whinging were most effective. I could wear down the toughest person by repeating ad nauseam what I wanted, why I needed it and how much it meant to me. It was an endurance sport I excelled at. I also learned to feign outrage and hurt on demand: 'It's appalling ...' 'It's disgraceful ...' Most of my customers were men so I used my body along with my intellect. I became what other women despise. Men were so malleable. I moved quickly through the ranks at Xerox. Pay was performance-related so my income rose and with it my power.

Then I got pregnant.

By this time Laurence had qualified as a barrister. We moved in different worlds. Yet our connection, made at a time when each of us was on the floor of our lives, was solid. We decided to keep the baby and get married. It was a small wedding held in his home town. His mother had the look of a woman biting on something sour. I remember my father, sitting outside the church on a low wall, cap on one knee, his tie and collar loosened, and the white of his scalp contrasting with his tanned forehead and red cheeks. All he was missing was a flask of tea, and a handkerchief on his crown with the four corners tied. I was a stranger to my mother. Once the ceremony was over, I used the excuse of pregnancy fatigue to escape both families.

Pregnancy suited me well until the sixth month. Then not only was my stomach extending but layers of fat were laid down over my arms, chest and thighs. I felt globular and amorphous, invisible to men. I had a disability; someone to be pitied or assisted, not taken seriously. I joined a gym, trained religiously and watched my food intake. By late pregnancy, it was me and baby bump with no extra bits. Iseult Matthews was born on a warm spring morning on the 5th of May. I left hospital as soon as possible. In the first week in the supermarket with her, as I reached for a packet of nappies I felt a tightness in my neck. I looked down at Iseult, asleep in her baby chair in the trolley. I felt pins and needles spreading up my arms to my face and around my mouth. I couldn't lift the nappies. I experienced an ominous feeling from the temperature of the air and the noise from the freezers that the roof was going to fall in. I wasn't frightened that I would die, only that she would. I grabbed the baby and ran out of the supermarket, leaving my shopping behind. It reminded me of the day when I was eight, I decided to walk home from school instead of taking the bus. At the foot of the mountains, the sky darkened. I thought the mountains were going to roll after me so I ran all the way home.

Within four weeks of the birth, although my stitches were just healed, I was desperate to make love with Laurence. It wasn't enough. When she was two months old, I asked Laurence to skip his Friday pint in the pub after work and come home early.

'We need to talk'.

After dinner I started.

'How long are we together now, Laurence?'

He shrugged his shoulders and squinted as he does when waiting for clients to confess.

'Five years? Six?'

'What's bothering you, Alice?' Normally he called me Ally.

'Well, I've been thinking. You know how couples seem to be close when their kids are small then over time they just get used to each other?'

'Jesus, Alice, you need to get back to work'.

'Hear me out, please. Look around'.

'What?'

'What happens? They grow apart'.

'That's life'.

'Then one person falls in love and the marriage is over'.

'Well that won't happen to us. So don't worry about it'.

'It won't?'

'Is that it? I want to see the match'.

He reached for the remote control and sat on the couch. I took it from him and sat on the floor, resting my chin on his knees.

'I've got a plan for our lifetime together'.

Laurence threw his body backwards and crossed his hands behind his head.

'Okay, I give up. Shoot'.

'It's very simple. I hate surprises. What I would like is for us to accept that at some stage each of us will fall in love with someone else'.

'Look, if you have an affair then it's over'.

'Is it? Does it have to be?'

'Jesus, are you saying that if I had an affair it wouldn't be? Come on, no way'.

'That's exactly my point. If either of us have an affair it will be a fling but that shouldn't change us; we can still be together afterwards, if we have some rules'.

'Rules?' Laurence's face flushed and he looked guilty. He often does when he is being truthful whereas he can lie and maintain a look of innocence.

'It depends on how you manage it. Anonymity and privacy; no names, no details and no stories back'.

'It's not going to happen'.

'Maybe. But if it does, do we have an agreement?'

'Whatever you say, Ally'. he reached for the remote control again 'whatever you say'.

I went upstairs to check on the baby.

After three months at home I arranged a sitter. I hoped to sever or at least temper my feelings for the baby. It was too overwhelming. I phoned from work hourly to hear how she was. My breasts pricked on hearing a baby cry in the street. Milk flooded my breast pads and blouse. Each evening I spent hours just looking at her, touching her, singing and playing with her. I scheduled trips away in order to wean myself off her. My boss considered this evidence of my commitment to my job. Colleagues at my level either did not have children or had wives to look after them. I maintained my hard-selling persona at work. My veneer of confidence held me together. Work was chickenfeed compared to home.

It's only when something happens you can see how stagnant life was before. Laurence had become wallpaper on the periphery of us. He had his first fling when Iseult was eight months. I have an aunt who judges character by people's responses to her cookery questions. She asks visitors what they like to cook and how. She watches to see if they'll bluff as she tracks them to the limit of their knowledge.

My first hint was when he suggested melting cheese over iceberg lettuce under the grill, a method new to our years of shared living. I sat at the table, the baby on my lap clapping, and watched him. This man had a spring in his step, a new haircut, a light in his eyes. He took long baths instead of showers. He dressed and undressed in front of the mirror with furtive glances at himself. He bought new clothes, new shoes, new underwear.

When he came home from an evening class, he carried the smell of a light musk. I pictured her instantly; bohemian, soft, ethereal. His antidote to me. The following week I parked down the street from his lecture hall. Sure enough, out he came with a fresh-faced young woman, auburn hair to her waist and long flowing skirts. They walked slowly away in step, close but not touching, except for their little fingers hooked together. Then he turned and pulled her into a doorway where they kissed. I drove home. That night, as I drew him to me and we made love, I decided to take the next step.

My opportunity came at the next conference. Fabio had slicked back hair, black down-sloping eyes and a tendency to over-explain himself. We fell into a pattern, meeting two or three times a year. All the pleasure of physicality without any of the ties.

In time Iseult grew into her own person and started school. She was a serious little girl; sensitive, organised and methodical. When she was nine she was being bullied by her classmates. They used to mimic and ridicule her. I bought her a boxer dog she named Wolf to distract her. Wolf was so happy that his whole body wagged. He was too powerful for us to walk. We employed a dog trainer who recommended using a choke collar.

'It will not damage the dog but don't look the him in the eye'. He said. 'And he won't know you're the one hurting him. He'll get the message and change his behaviour. Then after the walk you remove the collar and play. For optimal control you need the right balance of pain and play'.

When she was twelve Iseult went to boarding school. Laurence's good form sustained. As his 40th birthday approached, he enquired could an actor friend who was out of work, come to stay with us for a few months until her next job. I suggested she come to lunch the following Sunday.

Astrid was tall with long dry red hair and translucent skin. Tiny bells on her anklets tinkled like a cat as she walked. She was vegan so he prepared lunch, an avocado salad with seeds and pine nuts. Astrid brought a bunch of orange lilies, which I placed in a blue ceramic jug in the centre of the table. She ignored him and made small talk with me. Interesting, I thought, she's focussing on the decision-maker. He fussed over her. When she left I took a big bloody steak out of the fridge and fried it with onions. We ate it together. I agreed to his visitor staying if he would stock her odd food requirements and I would not have to curtail my meat eating.

Astrid contributed in unusual ways. Patchouli incense in the bathroom, pink flowering cacti in the kitchen and odd arrangements of leaves and stones in unlikely places. She fixed the broken banister, emptied the hoover and painted the back garden wall white. In the evenings she munched on fruit and grains as I ripped the flesh off chicken drumsticks or gutted and grilled fresh mackerel. If they were physically intimate they were discreet. It did not impinge upon me.

Everything changed when I broke my leg in a skiing accident. I was discharged from hospital with a metal plate in my shin, a plaster cast and instructions to stay off work for six weeks. Our days fell into a rhythm. We ate breakfast together, Astrid and I. Then she helped me bathe and dress. I parked on the sofa for the day with trade journals, my laptop and phone. I had no interest in work.

She did a stretching routine each morning to music. The sitting room had the best light for this so I had no objection to sharing it with her.

My body knew what was happening before I did. It started to wake me at five. Colours and smells became more vivid. Sounds sharper. Food tasted extraordinary though I couldn't swallow it. It was as though a plunger had been pressed up through my centre so I was always full. I felt restless. My eyes sought her constantly. When she left the room they lingered on her things. When I released my weight into the bath I could feel my back yearning to lean into her hand as she raised the sponge to squeeze water down my neck. When I ran my fingers over the inside of my lips I was convinced I was touching hers. Weeks passed. Weight I had been trying to shift for years fell from my bones. I was lean, pared down to myself, pure and urgent. My cast loosened on my leg. She asked why I no longer accepted her help. I didn't want her to see the raw need in my reduced body.

'I can't –'

She placed the pads of her four fingers on my lips.

'Come', she said.

She led me to her bed. My body had rehearsed this. Slowly she undressed me. I shook with each new touch. Then she stood to undress herself. My fingertips explored every part of her.

Starved for each other, we spent mornings in her bed. In the afternoons I pretended to read or work on my laptop while she read scripts and rehearsed lines. Her Patchouli smell on my fingers, her taste on my lips, my skin alight with the memory of her strokes. I had not known abandon like this before. I knew I'd be devastated when it would end, which it must.

A Kind of a Smothering

Dervla is most careful with patients she dislikes. Professionalism kicks in. She slows down her diction and takes care to be thorough, so her dislike does not influence treatment. She is the psychiatry senior house officer on-call tonight and across the table from her on a blue plastic chair, sits Micko, sweating and trembling.

'What age are you anyway, Doc? 26? 27? Sure you're only a kid'.

The walls of the Admissions room are painted in shiny magnolia and the floors are old parquet, some pieces loose. The smells of cabbage and French polish fill the air. Dervla writes in his chart.

'How much alcohol do you drink at the moment?'

'I haven't touched a drop today, Doc'.

His black hair falls forwards as if he has just lifted his head from a bucket of water. His sleeves are rolled to the elbow and a small comb protrudes from his back pocket

'A typical day in the last two weeks, say, give me an idea of your intake'.

'I'm not an alcoholic. Just a few benders, now and again. Same as any man. Well, any Irish man. She doesn't get it, though, no matter how many times I tell her, I can't get it through her thick skull'.

Dervla waits in silence. She has two different coloured eyes, one green flecked with brown, and the other brown. People usually look into her green eye.

'Where are you from anyway, Doc? Dublin? The Midlands? Are you long over here?'

Irish patients she comes across in London are always trying to get a handle on her. Where she's from, who her people are, whether they might know anyone belonging to her.

'Galway. I need to record your daily alcohol intake please. How much do you usually drink?'

'Galway, be dad. Not too far from my own place. From Tipperary I am. Grand spot, Galway. Well…' He flattens his fringe with the palm of his hand. 'On a good day, after my morning calls, I'll swing by the off-licence and buy a couple of bottles of Jack Daniels, if the expenses will stretch that far, mind. And that's me set up for the day'.

'Two 70cl bottles, is it?'

'Jesus, you haven't a clue, have you? Do you take a drink at all, Doc? This is crazy. Why can't I deal with the boss man? No offence Doc, but you wouldn't understand'.

She records two 70cl bottles in his chart, 56 units of alcohol per day, over three times the safe weekly limit.

'And on a bad day?'

'You didn't answer my question'.

His tremor increases. He sits on his hands in an effort to still them. Drops of sweat roll down his temples, down the side of his face, plopping onto the shoulders of his light blue shirt.

'Dr Turner will see you in the morning. It's my job to take your details and to prescribe some medication to make you comfortable tonight. Tell me about your bad day, please'.

'You can't imagine, Doc. I'm awake at four or five in the morning with nightmares, shaking and worried. I'm in the spare room now so herself doesn't hear me take the eye-opener. I sit at the side of the bed in my vest and boxers and take a few slugs. That tides me over until I leave the house at nine'.

'What do you do between five and nine?'

'I channel-surf on the TV or maybe go online. If I'm in bed I pretend to be asleep until she has the kids in the car for school. I can't stick them at all'.

Dervla is not looking forward to next year. As part of training, each of the psychiatry registrars will have to do one year's therapy. One to one, an hour a week. She'll have to cast a dragnet over her childhood and adolescence. She wonders what will this sift up. Will she become one of these snivelling people who recall every sideways glance or throwaway remark made by their parents? Or will she blame them or as is politely and lethally rephrased, 'acknowledge that inadvertently though they tried their best, they did cause her harm'? She thinks of her mother, up before dawn, frying bacon for breakfast, curls on her neck wriggling loose from her long plait. Or her father, coming in on a blast of sweet milk mixed with the smell of fresh cow dung, his wellies sitting with all of theirs on the back step. She thinks of Martin and the ease she has with him and whether that will survive all this probing. Every feeling scrutinised, every motivation explored.

She returns her attention to Micko Greene now at the end of his well-rehearsed litany of how life has dealt him a bad hand and sure, what can a man do. John, the psychiatric nurse for Ward 5, enters with the medication ready in a syringe. Micko brightens.

'Ah, Doctor, I was just saying to Doctor, em, Doctor '

'Dr Murphy?'

'Dr Murphy, the very one. I was telling her that I'd like you to have a look at me, check me over, like'.

'Mr Greene, I'm staff nurse John Taylor and I'll be giving you a little injection to ease the sweating. Dr Murphy is the doctor looking after you tonight. You'll see Dr Turner tomorrow, when she comes around'.

Dervla's bleep goes off. She phones Ward 7 from the Nurse's station. On the corridor she waves goodnight to John. Standing behind him, Micko looks like a lost boy. He carries his clothes bundled in an orange hospital issue plastic bag under his elbow. He waves back at her as he follows the nurse into the ward.

She walks down the steps and unlocks her car. It is a clear summer night and the old psychiatric hospital spreads out before her; red bricked Victorian buildings scattered around the grounds of what once was a lush estate. The day-patients look after the vegetable garden and the orchard where pear trees climb the high stonewalls. She sits into her old car, twists the key in the ignition, listens to the engine turn over and drives slowly to the ward.

Ward 7 is a locked ward at the hospital perimeter. She rings the bell and stands, breathing in the scent from the lavender plant at the doorway. A nurse she hasn't met before signals to her and unlocks the door with a key from his belt.

'Hilda Mills again?'

'Yes, sorry to call you out again, Dr Murphy. I just came on and she's at the top dose of her medication. It doesn't seem to have touched her'.

Dervla sits in the nurse's station and through a one-way mirror watches Hilda pace the adjoining assessment room. She is deeply tanned, not surprising with medicine-related photosensitivity. She has cropped henna-coloured hair, brown eyes and a glinting nose stud. She is talking, shaking her head and pulling at her fingers as though emphasising a number of crucial points. She presses her palm against the glass. The areas of contact blanche.

'I'll just have a word with her. Come in with me, please'.

They enter the assessment room and sit with their backs to the wall. Hilda continues to pace.

'The most important, the most, most, most important thing'. She turns quickly and moves her face close to Dervla's. 'Don't interrupt. I tell you. No interruptions. No teruptions. No putations. No tations, patiens. No!'

Spittle flies from her mouth landing on the floor between them. Hilda resumes pacing, and starts to move the grey chairs around the room to make each point.

'Hilda, my name is Dr Murphy, you may remember '

Hilda moves her face close again to Dervla's and whispers loudly at her.

'Murphy, smurfit, murfit, curfit, cunt!'

She paces again.

'You may remember we met the first night you came in here. You were upset and I gave you some medicine to help you get some rest'.

'Rest, pest, poison, in your veins, in your arteries, in the chambers of your brain, as you sleep, on the airwaves, caves, seas, rocking, boat, dead birds, dead rats…'

Hilda sits on the floor enumerating from her fingers in silence. Then she looks up and cowers, flinching, as though being hit from above. She holds her hands over her ears and rocks. Dervla and the nurse slip out of the room.

'I might have taken your word for it. I'll prescribe something more sedating'. She writes her up for additional medication.

'Thanks, Doctor. Have a good sleep. Hopefully that'll do it'.

The nurse accompanies Dervla out both sets of doors, unlocking and locking each as they go. She looks back as she walks to her car. He is still standing there, his face in the shade.

Hilda Mills. She presented her case at the regional meeting last month. A sprightly 45-year-old woman with three teenage boys. Ten months in the bath. Easy to understand how a person subject to a constant monologue from the devil could do this. His hot hand squeezing the back of her neck, synging her hair. *Echo de la pensée,* the devil echoing her thoughts. But her family. Bringing three meals a day to the bathroom door. Bringing her the phone. Keeping the hot water on through the summer. Not telling anyone. No visitors. Her husband thought it was just a phase, that it would pass. Her sister visited the house one day and insisted on seeing her. Only for that she'd still be there. What else was going on in that house while the children's mother was in the bathroom? It took six weeks as an in-patient for her skin to recover, as long to get her schizophrenia under control. Hilda never accepts her illness. On return home she stops taking her medication and gradually slides down into florid psychosis. Dervla isn't offended by the spitting venom Hilda shows her; it always disappears when she is well. So different from the aggression of alcoholics; that malice feels like it is part of their character, uncovered by alcohol, rather than part of the disease. Maybe she blames them for their addiction. That they have a hand in their own downfall hampers her compassion for them.

She drives across the grounds to the Doctors' Res. An arch of clematis with purple and white star-shaped flowers hoods the entrance doorway. Her shoes squeak on the polished parquet. She ignores the smell of toast and the murmur from her colleagues in the kitchen and goes to her bedroom. It is like a nun's cell, the height of the ceiling greater than the width of the room. Lit by a naked bulb, the walls are in baby blue gloss. The white metal base of the bed is two and a half foot wide. No danger of Martin sleeping with her here. If it were Ireland there would be a crucifix on the wall at the foot of her bed and nuns with steely whispers and soft-soled shoes, running the hospital. The bedside locker is standard hospital issue with just enough space to take the phone. The sheets and towels have NHS emblazoned across them; an enticement for junior doctors to steal them rather than a deterrent as intended. She undresses in the moonlight and gets into bed, leaving the curtains open and taking off her watch and engagement ring.

Last night she had a nightmare and in her sleep pulled off her ring. She had difficulty finding it in the morning. It was wedged in the corner of the duvet cover. In the dream she was instructed to dive from a height into a shallow pool. She was cautioned that there were chambers in the pool where she could become trapped. But, the instructor reassured her, we have a helicopter on standby for rescue, if necessary, he said. She worried about getting stuck in an underwater chamber from which the helicopter wouldn't be able to free her. She woke up sweating, listening to a woodpigeon cooing outside her window.

She rings Martin but there's no answer so she texts him goodnight. She slides down in the bed and feels her body twitch as sleep rises up to take her.

The bedside phone rings. It's John from Ward 5.

'Sorry, Dervla, were you asleep?'

She turns on the light to look at her watch. Midnight.

'A&E from UCH have been onto us. Another admission, I'm afraid. Attempted suicide'.

'What lovely things you bring me'. She yawns. 'How soon?'

'Funny thing is, some junior had this fellow admitted on the surgical side in UCH and then the surgeon, Mason, got wind of it and hit the roof. "I'll have no loonies on my ward. Get him out!" He's crossing the city as we speak'.

'That would be Mason, alright. Likes his patients in one or two dimensions only. Nice clean lines. No parallel worlds. So what did the patient do?'

'Attempted hanging I think, rope burns to the neck, no other injuries'.

'I'll be over at 12.30'.

She dresses in blue surgical scrubs and hospital clogs. Funny how surgeons always have strong names, Mason, Carson, Brown, Gilbert. Never any flowing loose endings. Finite and concrete. Nothing left to chance. In the kitchen she makes toast and coffee. She turns off the television. The empty pizza carton stuffed into the bin smells of gherkin and chorizo sausage.

In Ward 5 John nods at the couple seated outside the Nurses' station and hands Dervla the file.

'There's your man'.

She looks out at the couple. The man looks like Jesus. He is tall and lean, bearded with black glossy shoulder length hair and sad brown eyes. The woman is small with spiky blonde hair and big blue eyes accentuated by mascara and eyeliner. She is buxom, her jewelled navel just visible between her crop-top and miniskirt. She swings one foot, flapping a flip-flop up and down. The couple are engrossed in one another.

Dervla looks back at John.

'He's some tulip. I'll bring him in to the assessment room and ask her to wait so you can speak to her after'.

She shakes hands with the patient, Simon Wells, and introduces herself. He has a Geordie accent. The intensity of his eye contact is difficult to bear. She concentrates on her notes. He is very keen to tell his story so it doesn't take much probing. How he first met Colleen last summer at an open-air concert. How they moved in together in September, and are inseparable since. How devoted he is to her. Can't imagine his life without her. All the ways he loves her.

Dervla watches a serpentine vein on his left temple just visible under his sallow skin. She watches his Adam's apple rise and drop with his words, the two red rope burns on each side of it. His skin is sucked into the hollows above his collarbones. Nothing spare. She notices the curve of his deltoid and biceps under his loose white linen shirt. He is a carpenter. What else. She imagines him lifting her couch in one smooth movement and turning it upside down to examine the base. She imagines him lifting a door onto its hinges, wedging pieces of wood beneath to tilt it towards the frame. She imagines his flat abdomen and the curve of his oblique muscle proud above the pelvic brim. So here it is. So unexpected. Her capricious libido flexes itself. Desire. She's never found these big strong manly types attractive before. Must be the combination of his intensity, his romantic delusions and his vulnerability. The purity of Colleen, her beauty, the perfection of her voice, how she moves, and the ecstasy she brings him. He is raw need.

Dervla looks out at bubble-blowing Colleen, repairing her make-up and texting on her phone. Romantic love, that evolutionary device that throws people together who might never otherwise mate. She turns her attention back to Simon. There's something else. It seems to come off him in waves. Ah yes. Is it any wonder? An apple based scent, maybe his shampoo or soap, mixed with the smell of fresh sweat from a clean body. She's getting good at this. Maybe she won't need those one-to-ones after all. Or at least they won't throw up too many surprises. Now just a matter of locating that professional cover again, wherever it's gone.

'You've told me a lot about your happy times with Colleen. What happened tonight?'

'This last two months I've been getting so worried, so uptight about us. I'd be devastated if we split up. I'd be lost without her. She's my life. But I think she's tiring of me. I could see it coming'.

'You could see what coming?'

'She was going to leave me'.

She forces herself not to reply. Patients, when they are this earnest, find the most direct route to their truth.

'I love doing little things for her. I love being around her, sharing my life with her. But she's just been getting mad recently, saying she needs more space. I don't get it'.

'What happened?'

'She left a note for me. Said she was going for a drink with her mates after work and that she'd be home about ten. But I knew, you see, I knew that that's what she does when it's over'.

'How did you know?'

'I know everything about her. I know all her little secrets. I know her better than she knows herself'. He pauses and spreads his large tanned hands on the table, palms facing down, nails so flat they are almost concave. Dervla imagines placing a bead of mercury on each nail and watching it roll back and forth.

'I knew that for us to survive I had to prove to her that we're destined to be together. No good saying it. I had to show her. So. I didn't ring her, cos she was getting real narky about me ringing her during the day, at work and stuff. I texted her as usual, hoping she'd have a nice lunch, telling her I was thinking about her at 4 o'clock. Later wishing her a nice evening with her mates. And then at 9 o'clock I texted her to say to be sure to be home at 10, that I had a surprise for her'.

Dervla wonders does Martin ever think about her during the day.

'And that's when I did it. I had it all set up and ready. As soon as her key was in the lock, I kicked the chair out from under me and in she walked'.

'Did you want to die, Simon?'

'If I can't be with my Colleen, then yes is my answer'.

'You didn't want to die?'

'I wanted to prove to her how much I love her. That I'd give my life for her'.

'What did she do?'

'She's only a little thing, is Colleen, but she's strong, she is. She pushed the couch under me and grabbed me by the legs to take my weight and lifted me a little. Then I woke up'.

'How do you feel now?'

'Well, I'm glad it's all over. My neck's a bit sore. But I'm okay. As long as me and Colleen is okay, I'm okay'.

Colleen comes in on a blast of flowery perfume while Simon gives further details to the nurse outside.

'Hello Doctor, it's nice to meet you'. She offers her fingertips in the handshake. 'Sorry to put you to all this trouble, so late in the night and all'. She speaks in a guttural Liverpudlian accent.

Dervla starts a new page.

'He's mad, he is. Simon, like. He's really driving me mad. I've told him this is where we'd end up, I did. At the beginning I didn't know myself. Never had a man following me around adoringly, like him. You know? Well, I don't know if it's ever happened you, Doc, but it's very strange. He even likes the bits of me I can't stand. We all got them, haven't we? Never happy with the shape of me bum, I wasn't. Never liked it, plain and simple. Can't shut him up about it. The perfection of it. He'd wear you out. Then there's my toes. I have crooked fat little toes, I have. Never liked them. And I never wore high heels. Wouldn't break me bleeding feet for no one, I wouldn't. You know what he does? He buys this special foot oil and massages each one, kissing them in turn. I didn't know where to look. He's been getting worse too recently. Had to stop him phoning me at work. Now the texting's gone mad so that'll have to go too. Then last week he really frightened me. In bed we was, he grabs me by the face, his huge big hands holding my cheekbones and looks deep into me eyes saying, "No one will ever love you like I do. No one." Bloody hell. I thought to myself. I bloody hope not, neither'.

From her mobile phone comes a burst of baby's laughter. Colleen reaches for it and turns it off.

'Sorry, Doc, probably one of my mates. Worried sick about me, they are. Terrified they are, think he'll hurt me, though I don't think so. Himself he'll hurt. Look what he did tonight!'

'Were you planning to leave him?'

'To tell you the truth, Doc, I was. He's doing me head in. He's no fun anymore neither. You know yourself, with work and all, you need your rest. You need to be able to relax and have a few drinks with your mates, you know? Have a laugh?'

She pauses and runs her hands through her hair, her bracelets clinking with the movement.

'I do love him. You couldn't but. I mean in a way he's right. No one will ever love me in that way again. But when I met him I thought, now there's a big man. I mean look at the size of him, those shoulders. But he's not really, is he?' Her voice rises to falsetto. 'I mean one of my younger brothers is more of a man than him and half the size of him. He smothers me. That's it. It's a kind of a smothering, it is.

'What will you do?'

'I don't know, Doc, I really don't. I need my own space, I do. I'll get him home and we'll see. Look'. She passes Dervla a sheet of paper. 'What would you do if someone wrote that you?'

'My Dearest Colleen, you mean the world to me. Without you life is not worth living, my best love always, Simon. XXX OOO'

Dervla returns the suicide note. She thanks Colleen and advises her that Dr Turner will speak with them both in the morning.

She walks back to the Res. The moon is behind a bank of inky clouds now. She feels cool dew from the grass brush her bare heels. In bed her eyelids meet, like the magnetic close of a new kitchen drawer. She dreams that the walls of her room have writhing parts; elbows and knees protrude, like a body trapped behind a curtain, or a baby creasing his mother's stomach with a kick from within.

The following morning she reviews Hilda Mills before the ward round. The devil has left her alone for now. Though somewhat sedated, she responds to simple questions. Gone are the neologisms, the pressure of speech, flight of ideas and word salad.

On her way back to Ward 5, Dervla sees Colleen pulling up to the entrance in a pink Volkswagen convertible two-seater. Simon skips down the steps and climbs in over the door. They speed away, his hand on her shoulder.

Dr Jill Turner is sipping coffee at the Nurses' station waiting for the rest of the team to arrive. She has perfectly polished red nails and fleshy hands.

'Good morning, Dervla. You had a busy evening, I see'.

'Yes, Dr Turner, we had two late admissions. I just saw Simon Wells leaving with his girlfriend'.

'I had a chat with them both'.

'I thought he'd need to be kept in for a few days observation'.

'He wasn't depressed'.

'But his risk of self-harm'.

'Depression we can treat. But manipulation, the need to control others… we don't have any drugs for those'.

'Could we not give them counselling?'

'Certainly, if this was a man with good insight into his emotions and a willingness to work on his difficulties. But those who might benefit from our help, such as Simon and Colleen, often don't want it'.

'What'll happen?'

'That'll depend on Colleen. Some people like to feel needed that badly. It starts out sweet and intoxicating. Very addictive to feel that someone suffers for the lack of you. He's a limpet seeking a rock. The question is how long she is willing to be that rock'.

On her way home, Dervla stops at the beach. She watches the foam curdle on her feet as each wave sucks out and her feet sink deeper into the wet sand. She looks out to sea. Hard to believe it's the same water that washes up on Silver Strand or Coral Strand. When she goes home on holidays she often thinks she is going home to sanity. But that's not true either. In both lands it's the same water tide-marking the beaches, the same struggles people need help with. It just seems different here because the song of their stories sounds so strange to her ear.

Blind Spot

It started to snow at dusk and we travelled the last hour in silence, driving along the back roads with a few feet of white road visible ahead of us. The snowflakes melted when they touched the windscreen as if we had imagined them. We reached the farm and I lifted the stiff wooden gate. I stood holding it open while she drove through then I lifted it closed again.

'Oh, and one other thing', she said, as I settled back into the car, clots of snow falling from my coat. 'No touch'.

'What?'

'I mean it'.

'What?'

'No touching, hugging, kissing'.

'Who?'

'They can't stand it'.

'Can I shake hands?' I smiled.

'Yes, but not often'.

I looked over at her. She glanced at me then away.

A black and white sheepdog started barking as we pulled up in front of the whitewashed two-story farmhouse. The American custom of a Christmas wreath on the front door had reached even this part of Mayo. The heavy door was drawn open by a portly woman, her hair in curlers and flour on her navy and red apron. She rested her weight on her heels and folded her arms across her chest.

'And what kind of fuckin' four o'clock do you call this?'

'This is Gary I was telling you about'.

I put out my hand and she looked at it with disdain then back to my face.

'Not bad, Concepta'. She turned back into the house, muttering, 'Better than the last one'.

Connie turned to me.

'You've passed'.

We followed Mrs Devine into the big kitchen where she kneaded dough into submission on a large pine table.

The rigid compartments of our lives might have alerted me. Connie was available to talk to me only at specific times. Not during work hours. Not on evenings when she had classes. Never when she had arranged to meet with her friends. I also had times when I could not be reached. That left last thing at night, one or two nights a week. We had lunch together on Fridays and she stayed over with me on Saturday nights. If I contacted her outside of these times she didn't pick up or she spoke briefly and hung up. If I called to her place, she had a look of a trapped creature and immediately left the house on some pretext.

I won't lie. Our arrangement suited me well enough. I'd had my fill of clingy women, desperate for marriage, a child, or a social partner to buffer them from their patronising married friends or competitive workmates. To accompany them to work do's or weddings and to shield them from the goading remarks of family members. Those women wanted all of my attention and they usurped my leisure time with activities of little interest to me.

Our arrangement suited me well enough until I realised that that's all it was. Had I not met her family we might have continued on in that way, dandling pleasure, skirting commitment.

Dinner was almost without speech though not by any means silent. Connie's father nodded his acknowledgement of me as he dragged his heavy chair across the Liscannor floor into his place at the table. Jarlath, a cherubic form with red cheeks and a round bottom, copied his father's greeting to me. Connie sat opposite. She did not make eye contact and ate little. Mrs Devine slapped mountains of floury potatoes with slabs of bacon and scoops of cabbage onto each of the men's plates with half-portions for herself and Connie. She filled a fifth plate, covered it with a lid and left it heating on a pot of boiling water on the range.

'Will you spend Christmas with me?' Connie had said.

'Why wouldn't I?' I said.

'I mean in Mayo?'

'Why?'

'It's Christmas. It'd be nice'.

'But you don't get on with –'

'– It might be their last. You never know'.

She pulled the slide from her auburn hair. It loosened in folds down her neck, holding together in one loose sheaf, each rib of hair magnetised. Later we made love again, or what at that time I had thought was love.

Mr Devine and his son ate with their chins close to their plates. They loaded in mouthfuls of meat and vegetables then sat back to chew. Though their lips were closed, the sounds of crunching and grinding, followed by mashing and liquefaction dominated the room as frothy glasses of creamy milk fresh from the bucket were poured in on top of each mouthful until every liquefied load surrendered to being swallowed. Once their plates were clean of food, they mopped the remaining bacon juice with buttered bread, dabbing it delicately with their thick fingers and dropping it from above into their open mouths.

Sarah arrived, bustling into the kitchen, her arms full of presents. She dropped these on the couch and greeted each person in turn with a kiss on the cheek despite their best efforts to evade her.

'So'. She stood before me. 'You must be Gary. Delighted to meet you'.

I smiled, taking in her shiny eyes and warm hug. She looked at Connie.

'Where've you been hiding this one?'

'Where do you think?'

'Don't start, Concepta. Don't fuckin' think about it'. Mrs Devine doled out Angel Delight topped with tinned pears.

'They say', Jarlath said. 'They say it'll make great rain tonight'.

Everyone looked at him.

'Well, that's what I heard'. He blushed. 'On the radio, anyways'. He lifted his spoon and started scooping dessert into his mouth with magnificent sucking sounds.

'They do'. Mr Devine added. 'They do that. You know…' He began and glanced at his wife. She straightened in her seat and gave him a long look. He reached into his jacket pocket for his pipe. He cleaned out the bowl with his penknife, then struck it against the fleshy base of his thumb. He filled it with fresh tobacco, lit it and pushed his chair back. Puffs of indrawn smoke swirled past the unspoken sentence in his throat.

Connie had collected me from Furbo on that cold wet Christmas Eve. The back seat of her old black Saab was loaded up with wine, spirits and hampers.

'I didn't bring presents' I said.

'They don't expect anything from an impoverished writer'.

'Who'll be there, anyway?'

'My mother. Loves men, though she'll only show it by feeding you up. Signs on it when you meet Jarlath. Spoilt rotten though pushing fifty. Never left the nest. No woman ever doted on him like his Ma, nor ever will, looks like'.

'And Pops?'

'Won't say much. Likes his jar. His peace and quiet. He might share a joke with you, but only out of earshot of my mother. It's a sight to see him cry tears of mirth on his third pint'.

'And your sister ?'

'Sarah? She'll grace us. More's the pity. Hard work'.

'Oh?'

'Has to beat me on everything. She'll torture us with her good cheer and make a beeline for you'.

'Me?'

'A charm attack'.

'How long?'

'Two nights max'.

Sarah pulled up a chair and set down her dinner plate next to mine.

'So, Mam tells me you're a writer, Gary'. Sarah was an animated version of Connie; plumper, smaller, cuddlier, sparklier, warmer, safer.

'I –'

'– What do you write?'

'Books'. Said Connie crashing her dishes onto the sideboard in the back-kitchen. 'He writes books', came her disembodied voice.

'Well, of course, I didn't mean ... I mean, what kind? Have I seen –'

'– I have a novel coming out next year'.

Mrs Devine turned from the range where she was stirring custard.

'What's it about ... this novel?' Writing clearly wasn't a real job.

'It's a story, about a family'.

'A family?' Said Jarlath.

'A family ... I made up'.

'A family'. He said again.

'See, the family lose a baby and the story is about them coming to terms with that'.

'What do you mean 'lose' a baby?' Said Jarlath.

'The baby dies'. Said Connie, returning to her seat with a mug of coffee.

'Well, why didn't he say that then? Lose a baby, Jesus. As if you'd leave a fuckin' baby in a hedge or it'd fall out of the car or something'.

Everyone looked at Jarlath and he blushed again.

'That's very exciting, Gary. I'll look forward to reading it'. Said Sarah.

'Nah, nah, nah, nah'. Connie singsonged in the same tune as Sarah's voice, tipping her head from side to side. 'Nah, nah, nah, nah'.

'What's eating you?'

'You give me a pain in the tit'.

'Concepta!' roared Mrs Devine. 'To your room. Now!'

Connie giggled and fled upstairs with her mug, repeating her head movements at Sarah before closing the door. Mrs Devine piled three more potatoes onto my plate with the closest she could get to a smile.

My world divided that night into before and after.

Before, what people said is what they meant. Their hearts or bodies didn't harbour other motives. Those who loved, loved. In a one or two-dimensional simple way. It was boring. It was safe. But it wasn't an edifice for some other means, some other end.

After, there was no knowing. Words spoken were a loose interpretation of intent, only after they had passed through a sieve of acceptable responses. That filter yielded neutral language which voice inflexion, a look or body twitch could give any number of further meanings to.

That was her, Connie, the person I knew most intimately and yet not at all. It was me also, it emerged, a stranger to myself.

When Connie returned, I was sitting on the couch, wedged between the softness of Jarlath and Sarah, a hot whiskey on my knee, my feet resting on the fire fender, my socks starting to singe.

'One last check on them calves'. Said Jarlath.

As he stood the leather cushion made an unpeeling sound as it released him as though it had had contact with his bare flesh, not his shiny work trousers. He pulled on his wellies and left. Connie took his place. Now I was slouched between Connie and her softer double. The flesh at Sarah's waist embraced my right elbow. My left was in light contact with the top of Connie's slender hip. Desire seeped through me the way blood reperfuses fingertips on coming in from the cold. Connie stretched and reached for her father's wellies and overcoat.

'I'm off for a walk. See you later'.

She looked at me and I knew this was my cue to join her but I didn't.

When I climbed into bed, Connie turned away from me. A homemade patchwork quilt and three blankets weighed us down. It required effort to lift my ribs to breathe. I felt my limbs pressed into the mattress. I placed a hand on her shoulder.

'Get off'. She said.

'What?'

She turned to face me.

'Have her. I don't care'.

'Jesus, that's sick'.

'I know you, Gary. I won't have sex with you while you think of my –'

'– I'm not –'

'– Liar'. She brought her hand to my groin. 'That didn't happen just now'.

'You're unbelievable. Jesus, I'm not a lab rat with every erection accountable –'

'It'll end our little arrangement of course. But I was tiring of it anyway'.

'It's not like that and you know –'

'– My little sister played her card and you liked it. Bully for her. She gets the prize. Hooray, joke's over'.

'Is that what –?'

'– Look, who cares what you want to call it, it's over'.

I rolled onto my back and slid down so that the blankets covered my bare shoulders. The weight of the blankets forced my toes to point. It reminded me of Irish dancing class at school, the girls pointing their toes so the front of their ankles was flat, convex even, making a straight line from knee to big toe.

One night a week, one meal a week. This was no way to love. Parcelled. Intimacy by instalment. An avoidance really it was, a buffer against love. Just like the eye does with its own blind spot. It fills it in so well that it's hard to convince people they have a blind spot at all until you prove it by blindfolding one eye. I once spent a summer as an assistant at an Eye Clinic. They gave me a job mapping the hole in patients' vision on a blackboard. You measure its shape and dimensions and from that extrapolate the size of the actual blind spot at the back of the eye. Once the cover on the other eye is removed, the brain fills in the missing part with an image from the uncovered eye. Like the blank piece you might place in a jigsaw so there's no gap, your mind fills in the blank, yet knowing it's a blank, so you can see the overall pattern. However the blank isn't real, of course. It just keeps us moving. So we don't see the hole in our lives. Unless we choose to.

I felt her awake beside me. The room smelt of damp plaster and the deep cold you get from the walls of an old house.

My lips could still taste the peach-flavoured lip-gloss from Sarah's kiss. It had started as a brush of lips but my tongue couldn't resist probing inside to the place where wet starts. My thumb and finger had twirled in small circles on the skin of her waist. Circles like mirror writing as if I could feel it being inscribed concurrently on a conscious surface in my brain. I could have continued that caress forever.

As for our bodies, I had assumed that Connie's body spoke to me honestly but I was wrong. It had addressed me impersonally as the man in her life. I was the man it made love to. The man it showed affection to. As personal as her toothbrush. A utility. Something you need but that can be replaced easily if necessary. Maybe her face cleaned of make-up and smelling of toothpaste and night cream, breathing into mine at night, maybe it was another mask, a mimicry of wholesomeness and homeliness that didn't exist. And the clinch of her thighs around my hips, the urgency in her eyes as she pinned me down and I plunged into her, why did I assume that that had any connection with feeling for me? Why did I assume that this was personal for either of us? It was as though there was some part inside her that was not conducting heat or feeling, that had turned to wood. It was arbitrary. I was arbitrary. Any man would have done. Interchangeable, we were, we bent to her needs and fitted them to varying degrees. We took our pleasure and she hers. It went no deeper. It used the language and movements of love but it was bleached clean of it. I was her love object, her idea of love, not particularly liked, often endured but certainly not loved. And she was mine.

When Connie's breathing settled into the rhythm of sleep, I slipped out of bed and dressed in the dark. The kitchen was warm and smelled of turf. The fire embers still cast shadows on the walls. I collected my things and left. The sheepdog watched me and didn't bark.

On the main road, snow crunched under my boots and lit up the outline of the hedges and the stone walls. In the village I was lucky to hitch a ride back to Galway with a passing ambulance. I spent Christmas day thinking about the main character for my next novel, a man who lives three different lives in one. He moves between compartments, playing a different character in each world. On moving from one to the next he quickly forgets the previous life.

Bail Bonds

You got trouble with the law and you don't want to spend time in jail waiting for your case? Damn right you don't. So you come to us. Well, you've come to the right place. I'm Marlene and I'm the clerk at the front desk. I wasn't always a clerk. I am a fully-trained bookkeeper, got my diploma and all the papers to prove it. But that isn't a job for someone like me. I'm sociable and it was too lonesome. Stuck in a poky office with no window, no light or air. Writing in numbers and adding them up, filling in forms and writing pay checks for people I don't ever meet. After two weeks I realise I'm good at it but I hate it. So I amn't staying there any longer.

Then I was passing this place one day and I seen the advert in the window. I took me a look around it. Big tinted glass window out front so you can't see any one inside. Pavement all neglected, cardboard boxes, dirty take-out cartons. All the other stores and offices in the neighbourhood, they got steel shutters. Need them too. But not this one. It's open twenty-four/seven. It isn't a dangerous neighbourhood. I'm not saying that. But it's in that lost place, that no man's land. Not red light, not junkie, but no middle-class people living around here neither. So it isn't taken care of. Smell of petrol and tyre rubber in the air, even in the mornings. No grass, trees or parks to change that air, I suppose. There's a graveyard at the end of the street though. But that's fence to fence with graves and the headstones are placed flat on the earth so there's little space for grass to grow, just ivy on the wall and it clinging to the black wrought iron gate.

I stepped inside the office and jumped when the spring on the door slammed it shut behind me and a loud buzzer went off. The tinted windows made the office darker too. The people waiting on the bench were sure edgy; biting their nails or rubbing their knees. No question who was next in line to go see old Luke because they were pacing up and down.

I could see why they needed a new clerk. Old Luke sitting behind the security glass, he moved real slow. Could hardly hear neither. Had to ask every question twice. Clients ended up shouting their answers. They weren't too comfortable with that. We're not talking about some wedding list or wish list. This isn't a place you order a takeout coffee and a bun. This is no bucket list. This is your darkest nightmare. This is the thing that happens that's so bad you want to die. You don't want to tell nobody about it. And when you have to, then you don't want to shout it, no, you want to whisper it. Then you want to run away.

Next thing Roy comes out of his glass office at the end of the counter and strides over to old Luke. Roy's real tall, got a long nose with a bump on it and sticky-out ears. His eyes are close together and have that look like he knows all your secrets. He's the right one for this job. He has a way about him as if he's some kind of a monk. As if he's never been with a woman, though he's too old not to. He collects some files from old Luke then he signals to a client, an old guy with white shoes, to follow him to his office. He opens the glass door and white shoes walks in ahead of him.

Before Roy disappears I call him.

'Excuse me, Sir, I want to apply for the job you got advertised in your window'.

Everyone turns to look at me like why on earth would I want to work here but they don't know the kind of place I left. He smiles and comes loping down to shake my hand. His hand's big and the skin's dry. He's got white teeth but they're so small they look like baby teeth and that surprises me.

'Yes, Ma'am, I'm still looking. Let me get you an application form'.

Well, I fill in that form and Roy interviews me the following week. He asks some funny questions. He asks about my husband and if I've got children. Now I know them questions aren't legal but he's well-meaning so I answer.

'My husband's a carpenter, works for himself. He hasn't ever been in trouble or nothing. We got one child, she's nine'.

He brings up his index finger and thumb and he squeezes the bump on his nose, sliding that pinch down till it comes right off the tip.

'How would you feel, Marlene, about talking to a client who might have just committed a murder?'

I think about that and I don't rightly know how to answer.

'Well, sir, I don't see that it'd be my job to judge. They're going to court and the judge'll decide. I sit behind security glass, so I'm safe. And anyway, they're not guilty till the judge say so'.

He looks at me and his eyes smile so I know it's the right answer. He pinches that nose again.

'And what about if a man is up for raping a child or say, killing a child?'

I take a deep breath and let it out slow. No point lying to those eyes.

'Well, that'd be hard. Can't pretend otherwise. Course I'd want to kill him, who wouldn't? But I'd do my job. I think I would, do it right'.

He must have been happy with that because I started the following Monday. After all those questions I expected to spend my days talking to thieves, rapists and murderers. But of course that's not how it works. They're in jail, waiting for bail. I deal with the people that love them. Their mothers, their fathers, their sisters or brothers. Their children or their best friends. They're still ashamed though they did nothing wrong. They're ashamed that someone they love is in jail. They're ashamed that they have to talk to me and Roy about it. They don't have the money to pay for bail because they're poor or the crime's so bad it's a lot of money.

Calling to the Bail Bond office is like visiting the funeral parlour when your loved one dies. What size coffin do you want? What kinda wood do you want to house the body in? You want the basic model or all the frills? How much you going to pay? When do you want the body released? How much do you love him? Do you still love him? It's a test. It drives the reality home. It's hard.

I get to ask the easy questions. Name, address, contact numbers. The name and address of the person needing bail if it's different. Their social security numbers. What they plan to offer in terms of property or collateral to secure the bond. I've got one hard question to ask. What is the nature of the alleged offence. That question usually hits them. It's a warm-up for what Roy's gonna ask.

Roy's job's harder. He has to get to know them better. He's got to make sure their security's worth what they think it's worth before drawing up the contract. He has to find out more about the accused too. Roy's got a conscience. He's gotta make sure the accused's gonna show up for court. Sometimes there'll be screaming coming from that glass office of his. A woman wailing like she's been knifed. Maybe that's why this office wall's glass so everyone knows Roy's done nothing wrong. Maybe she's not able to believe anything else bad about her beloved even though he's already in jail. She's wanting to put their family home as collateral and Roy won't let her. Maybe the accused has a history of skipping bail. The accused is lying to the woman but she don't want to know. Roy knows. Roy's not making babies and sharing a life with the accused. He's seen it. The man skips, Roy's got six months to catch him and get him before the judge. Roy gets a Fugitive Recovery Company to track him and get him back. All that costs money, her money. She loses her home.

The rich, they're more complicated. It's a greater fall for them.

Take that case I had last Thursday, I clock in at 6 am, working the early shift. I bring out the trash ready for collection and pile it neat on the kerb. No cartons or rubbish around this office front no more. Orange streetlights flicker with the brightening sky, like turning the gas down on the stove.

Waiting are the usual clients. Two bums who come in from the cold. Hurting no one so I don't move them on. Their dirty hands wrapped around styrofoam cups of coffee, they blow steam off before sipping.

Next to them is a girl. Could be a hooker. She's young, wearing a lot of make-up, chewing gum and turning the magazine pages too quick.

Next to her is a rich one. Well, maybe not rich but she doesn't belong here. Her hair's ash blonde and blow-dried so it curls in neat, makes a straight line at the back of her neck. She's got big eyes and they're bigger again with those false lashes and eyeliner. Other people probably think she's got long lashes but I can spot the stick-ons. Had botox too. Anyone sitting on that bench without worry lines, they're botoxed or else they're deranged. Navy jacket fits just so. The waistline gives it away; she's a tall woman like me, even without those heels, and the tuck of her jacket hits her waist exactly. It doesn't ride up her back like some cheap garment from Kmart. Her face, it's shiny from expensive night cream. Her white blouse, it's busy with ruffles, covering belly fat would be my guess. Navy pants neatly ironed and the hem finishing just short of the ground. She's perched on the edge of the bench looking like she's the accused. It's her turn and she approaches the counter, laying down her clutch purse and a bunch of car keys, flashing her big rings.

'Can I help you, Ma'am?'

'I'm here to organise bail for my husband'.

I open a new file on the computer. Sure glad I got my nails done yesterday.

'His name please'.

'Peter. Mr Peter Miller'.

She answers all the easy questions. Now we get down to business.

'Can you tell me please, Ma'am, what is the nature of the offence your husband is accused of?'

That botox hasn't worked. This trauma's bigger than botox. Between her eyebrows a patch of muscle still pulses and clenches.

'Sexual assault'.

'Sexual assault', I repeat. 'Is that of an adult or a child? A male or a female?'

She's sweating now on her upper lip and forehead. She takes a swig from her water bottle. It snaps back and whistles as it refills with air as if it objects to her sucking on it. Her mouth still sounds dry when she speaks.

'Excuse me ... It's a child. Well, he's 14'.

I look up at her from my typing. She takes a deep breath again, looks like she keeps breathing in but not letting any air out.

'Sexual assault of a male child. Oh my God, I can't ...' She starts crying, rings and bracelets clinking, she's dabbing her eyes. She has it under control in about ten seconds flat and looks back up at me.

'Do you need anything further from me?' She asks as though I just slaughtered all her children.

'No Ma'am', I say. 'I'll just explain the process to you and then Mr Roy Barnes, sitting in that glass office over there, he'll talk to you some more'.

When we're done she says nothing, just sits on the edge of the bench, her back straight, her feet together, her eyes staring at the floor. She jumps when Roy calls her. Then she looks around quick, checking who's heard her name called out loud. No one cares. No one but her. She marches down to Roy and he holds the door open for her like he always does.

I'm glad I got this job, not Roy's. I don't have the feeling Roy's got for these people. He cares. He pretends no one's guilty. He pretends no one's capable of doing nothing bad. They're guilty. Course they're guilty. Lots of them's guilty. Their families should feel ashamed for the bad things they do. It does reflect bad on them. No changing that.

When people are hurting they want to hurt someone back. They've got to deal with us whether they like it or not. They need us. But that don't mean they've got to like us. It's a good reason not to. We're strangers and we're witnesses to this hard time in their lives. We're in on their darkest secrets and we're not welcome. So there's no way they're going to like us. But it's not personal, not really. Just human.

I am not heartless. I know they're in jail until the court case. Whether we bail 'em and send 'em home or we don't, they're in jail in their minds anyway and that's longterm. They suffer and their loved ones suffer until their sentence is read. It doesn't stop there neither.

Displaced Air

Laura watched Cillian in the rear-view mirror. From his child seat, he held one hand close to the roof of the car, a parachute hanging from pursed fingers, the other hand dandling his Action Man in his lap. Friday. Changeover day. More like give-away day. 'So, what will you do with Dad this weekend, Cillian?'

'He's not your Dad'.

'What'll you do with Mark?'

'Dunno, maybe the rides or the cinema'.

'Sounds great'.

She turned the car into the estate and glanced back at him again. He had stopped playing and was looking ahead, his glassy green eyes focussed in the distance.

'What'll you do, Mammy, and me gone?'

'I've lots of boring adult things to do, don't you worry'.

'Will you have long talks on the phone?'

'Definitely, and long boring walks too'.

'Don't do any of the fun stuff until I get back'.

'I won't bake chocolate Rice Crispies without you so and I won't go feeding Bernie's rabbits either. Can I do the hoovering?'

'You can do the hoovering'.

Her car pulled up outside a semi-detached house with a playhouse in the front garden.

'Private or public?' she asked.

'Private'. He said, opening his seatbelt and clambering out of his seat. He slid onto her lap. Her arms encircled him. She savoured the hold of his solid little body and its heaviness pressing against her. He hadn't yet learned to hold back.

A steady tapping on the window interrupted them. Ross, a neighbour who worshipped Cillian, was hammering his Action Man on the car window. He fixed his brown eyes on Cillian and continued until Cillian opened the car door and jumped out.

Laura carried Cillian's weekend bag to the front door and rang the bell. It was a busy estate, so different from her apartment block where there was no one his age and most people were at work all day.

'Get the door, will you, Mark?' a woman's voice called through the upstairs window. Then a clumping sound on the stairs. The door opened.

'Oh, hiya'. Tina wore heavy eyeliner and her baby, held in the crook of her arm, sucked on plastic keys.

'Hiya Cillian' she shouted and turned to Laura. 'Why don't I take that bag. Mark'll be down in a minute. Will you come in?'

'No, no, I'm grand'.

Laura watched her son play with his friend. The action man could fit through the chimney of the playhouse but the parachute got caught. They tried to bunch it and stuff it through.

'Hiya Laura', Mark said. 'Everything okay?'

'He's great, no problem'. Her eyes were on Cillian. 'His inhalers and tablets are in his bag'. She looked at Mark. 'See ya Sunday at six so'.

'He'll be fine, don't worry'.

'Course'. She half-smiled and walked to the car with her head down. Cillian looked up when the engine started. She waved at him. He shouted some instruction at Ross. Mark's hand tousled Cillian's hair as her car pull away.

Now what, she thought. Tidy the apartment, put away all his toys. Make the space as if he was never there, as if she was young and single and childless again, as if her life was all ahead of her like a patterned carpet waiting to be rolled out. She always intended to do that. To finish out each space of her life so each was lived in fully. But it didn't work. The one time she cleared away all evidence of him from the apartment, she felt wretched as though he had died, as though she had killed him off. So now she tidied his toys into his timber box leaving her favourites on top. She arranged his teddies all around his pillow so they were waiting for him.

'Did ye miss me?' He asked them in a high squeaky voice.

'Of course we did'. They answered in the deepest voice he could muster. 'Bored out of our skulls, we were, without you'. Then he dived in and returned his room to its usual chaos.

Meals were difficult without him. Before Cillian she had shared a house with friends so other people were always around, people to share cooking with, people to go out with without having to make an arrangement ahead of time. She still wasn't used to cooking a nice meal for one. Where was the pleasure in it? Even if she spent much of their mealtimes correcting him – he liked to walk around the kitchen talking as he ate, fingering his food and inevitably spilling it – he was still company.

In life before Cillian, Leonie owned the house and a gang of them sublet from her. She had made things very clear once Laura told her she was pregnant.

'Look' she said, curling her hair behind her ear with her index finger. 'I've just got a promotion. I worked bloody hard for that. I'm sorry but – '

'I get it'. Laura cut in. 'It wouldn't be fair. I've plenty of time to find a place'. Easier to soften the blow by receiving it rather than wait for it to land.

'I'm really sorry. I'll help you out in any other way I can. Really, I will'.

And she did. Flowers at the birth. Baby blankets. Dimplex radiators when the heating broke down. She was a good pal. Up to a point.

Laura drove out of the estate. The car ahead braked then beeped and drove on. A young man in the white tracksuit and a peaked hat meandered in the middle of the road in the way of traffic. He couldn't have been more than nineteen. His eyes were half-shut. She pulled in to the kerb, got out of her car and waited for the traffic to pass.

'Excuse me!' she called. He looked over at her and waved as if to bat her away. 'Come in off the road! You'll be killed'.

He replied in a foreign language and staggered on. She ran out, grabbed his arm and forced him towards the path. He squinted at her, his eyes sliding sideways.

'You can't walk on the road like that. It's too dangerous!'

'I sorry'. He said, through his mouth of black teeth. 'I sorry, lady. No harm. Please'.

He wavered, drifting toward the wall.

'What is your name?'

'Kazik, my name'.

'And where are you from, Kazik?'

'Poland, I from Poland'.

'Let me drive you home. Where do you live?'

'I no English. I with friend'.

'Ring your friend. They tell me address'.

'No credit. My phone kaput'. He lifted his phone and laughed while he drew his finger across his throat.

'Come to my car'.

She took him by the elbow and they lurched to her car, Kazik in turns walking unaided then leaning on her. He slid into the passenger seat. She handed him her phone. He was too drunk to key in the numbers so he called them out to her, reading them from a slip of cross-hatched paper. Once she heard a ringtone she passed it back to him. He spoke in Polish.

'Does he speak English?' she asked.

Kazik hung up, 'Ballybane Industrial Estate. Tomasz meet'. The car filled with the glue-like smell of exhaled alcohol.

Once traffic was clear, she turned the car around and drove the two miles over to Ballybane. The industrial estate was deserted, the shop-front shutters pulled down, typical for a Friday evening. She parked and waited.

'My friend, he come'.

'When did you come to Ireland?'

'I one week in Ireland. One week'.

'What kind of work do you do?'

'Oh, you nice lady. So kind'. He grabbed her left hand and shook it, trying to pull her towards him.

'No, no', Laura laughed. 'It's okay. You don't need to do that. Thank you but no'.

'So kind'. When he couldn't hug her he held her hand and started to kiss the back of it, his own finger nails bitten and dirty.

'Please', she smiled, trying to pull away. 'There's no need, really. Let go now'.

He kissed her hand again then let her pull it back.

'So Kazik, what work do you do?'

'Electrician'. He pulled off his peaked cap. A long white scar on his scalp ran from forehead to crown. The rest of his head was shaved. No hair grew on the scar. He squeezed the hat visor so it made a cone and sudden tears fell onto the backs of his hands.

'Are you okay, Kazik?' it was getting darker outside and few cars passed.

'Bad things. In Poland. Police. In trouble'.

He looked across at her, his eyes all pupil.

'It's okay, Kazik. Don't worry. It'll be okay'. She reached to rub his arm. He jerked away, put his cap back on and curved his body towards the door. She pressed redial. When he heard the ring tone he turned and snatched it from her.

'You phone police!' he shouted, swinging his fist back in readiness to strike her.

'No, Kazik. I phone Tomasz. Please give me phone. I speak'.

He checked the number and returned it to her.

'Hello, I am Laura. I have Kazik. You come to Ballybane?'

'No. I late. Meet at Trapper's Inn. Better'.

'Okay. I drive to Trapper's Inn now. Five minutes, okay?'

He hung up.

Laura drove while Kazik sat quiet, a hunched, clenched bulk beside her.

In the Trapper's Inn car park, a small man built like a wrestler, got out of a 2001 Audi. Two other men remained inside, speaking on mobile phones.

Tomasz walked over and admonished Kazik in Polish. Kazik removed his hat and cowered. Tomasz turned to

Laura, placed his hands on his hips and tipped his head back and looked down at her. Although he was smaller than her he looked taller. Laura was glad she had not understood the exchange.

'So what you want lady? You want money?'

'Kazik was walking in the middle of the road. He nearly got killed. So I gave him a lift'.

Tomasz spun around, roared in Polish at Kazik then struck him on the side of the head with his fist and the youth fell to the ground. Tomasz stood over him, nudging him with his foot and shouting. Kazik scurried over to the Audi and climbed in.

Tomasz pulled a roll of fifty-euro notes out of his pocket, removed the brown elastic band and started to pull off fifties.

'Kazik a bad boy. Stupid. I pay you, lady. No problem.

Laura raised both hands and backed away.

'No. No money. Please. I'm happy he's safe'.

He stood with his arms crossed and watched her drive away.

Outside the apartment her arms were still shaking. She thought about Cillian's dreamy. If he was upset about school, missing his Dad or being sick, he always asked for his dreamy.

'Okay'. She said each time. 'All boys and teddies take positions'. He galloped into his bedroom, flung himself on the bed, kicked off the pillows and duvet and lay flat on his back with his teddies curled under his arms.

'Ready to launch'. He shouted. Laura crept into the room, listening for his stifled chuckles then she admonished the teddies with her giving-out face while theatrically placing her ciúnas finger on her lips.

'Silence, teddies! Dreamy is a serious business'. More suppressed giggles.

She raised the top sheet by both corners and lifted it in one swinging movement so it spread and landed over the child's head and body. Next the repeated whipping motion by raising the end of the sheet with straight arms to send a wave of light and air and wind up the bed so that momentarily she saw Cillian's face filled with glee until the sheet lowered again to cover him, leaving his profile, a caricature of him viewed from above. He accompanied these cycles of light and dark, breath and feathers, with giggles and chortles and they ended only when Laura's back and arms tired.

Once home she climbed into Cillian's bed and snuggled all the teddies around her head like he did. She looked up through the velux window at the grey sky and watched light rain touch the glass then stream down. Drops that coalesced gained more momentum and reached the base sooner. The rain stopped and the cloud cover parted. She fixed her eyes on the patch of blue and noticed the floaters in her eyes streaming with each saccadic eye movement. You could only see floaters if you focussed in the distance and expected them to drift across your field of vision. Floaters moved at the same speed as the sheet when after being whipped high in the air, it displaced air slowly and landed lightly on her son's giddy body.

McGurl

Fidelma McGurl, that's my name. No one but teachers calls me that and lives. McGurl my friends calls me, Fiddler for short.

Fiddler lobs the ball into Torres, he kills it, spins it over to Kuyt, quick pass back to Fiddler, unmarked at the edge of the box, a powerful left footer into the right corner of the net. What a goal! Manchester's goalie, Van Der Saar, stares at me, the whites of his eyes showing. The strong left foot. Always catches them. Brill. I tear around the pitch, my two spindly arms in the air and fists clenched, Cuyt and Torres trailing after, slapping my back. The crowd roars 'Liverpool …' Sweet.

It's six thirty in the morning and my clock is about to go off. I hit it before it does. Mikey is mooching about next door. I hear him breathing his queer little snuffles. I sneak in, drag him out of bed where he's curled next to Brenda, like one of them cocktail sausages stuck to each other, and carry the warm bundle of him in my arms down the stairs. He's glassy-eyed for the first half hour so I pour his Cheerios and eat my breakfast while his brain warms up. Mikey is the best of them. No guff. Never needs a clip on the ear. He has them slanty eyes like you do see in them posters at the bus stop. We could do with more of that. I like having breakfast with Mikey. I slip on my work gear, grab my training gear then scatter before them others start arsing around the house.

'Where's my shoes? Where's my school bag? Who took my hairbrush? Who swiped my go-go's?' Don't know how Ma sticks it.

Me and Mikey's a team. We go places, don't we, Mikey? His eyes sparkle back like two bulls eye sweets someone's licked. It's Monday morning. All my mates'll be dragging themselves to work. Not me. We won the big one on Saturday. The under 21's Connaught Club Finals. We's going places now. No stopping us. All Irelands next. And then what? Who knows, maybe one of them scouts'd spot me. Never know your luck.

'The stars', coach says, 'the stars is the limit if you've got the right attitude'.

I'm out the door after a big smackeroolie for Mikey. I love the smell of sleep on his neck when I squash him to me. Little boy sweat, smells like lollipops, it do. At the end of the road I wait for the seven-fifteen bus. Who'd a thought. I reckoned my career was over when I landed in this dump. My Ma thought we could all do with a change after me Da dying and all. Three year ago now. Applied for one of them council swapamajigs. Never thought she'd get it.

'Who in their right mind'd want to live in St Teresa's Gardens?' says I.

Jesus, someone did. Fucking eejits. So we landed up here. Thought it would be a right royal place when we heard the address. Castle Park indeed. Sure it's more of the same. No question. Just scattered over more ground, is all. And a few piebalds thrown in. The people is culchies too of course. But it's the same knackers messing up the place during the day. The same car racers scaring people in their beds be nights. I do worry about Mikey, I do. Make me Ma promise she'll keep him in after the tea, at least till I get back after training. She says she will if she's there. By this she means if she's not sloshed down in the local. Doesn't like it when I says that out loud. Doesn't like it at all.

'You'll see'. She says. 'You'll see what it's like when you've a few screamers of your own'.

I don't answer. I don't tell her. Be afraid to. Put a jinks on it, it might. In case I don't manage to pull it off, like. Sometimes I'd be thinking if I don't say it, then there's still a chance.

'A better life'. She said. 'We'll have a better life in the west'.

In some ways she was right. Bagser, for instance. He's a great fella. Drives around the estates every evening picking up girls for training. For nothing, like. I mean it. You'd have to see him of course to know what I mean. Jam jar glasses you can't see his teeny eyes through, not a hair on his head to speak of and roly poly from the cheeks down. Big t-shirts and track suits. Not exactly a girl's wet dream. At first I thought what's this fella playing at? What does he get back for all his taxi-ing? Thought he'd be gunning for the quick feel, the hand on your bum, the grab in your crotch, squashing against your boobs to pass you in the changing room. But no. He's a good fella, he is. Maybe he'd never get talking to girls if he didn't do this. Maybe that's it. I don't know. What I do know is he's getting these girls off the streets. Giving them a love of football. And that's something.

'It's not natural'. My Ma says. 'Not natural, at all. A young one like you should have a fella. You got a job now. You should be settling down. Instead of following a ball around and around'.

'Yeah, Ma'. I don't answer. 'Yeah and before I'd know it, preggers, then a flat, then whinging all my life at him to be getting stuff for me. Me and the baby. No thanks'.

Saw a documentary once on the telly, flicking around during the Corrie ads, I was. Women in Africa, cut off one boob to shoot their bow and arrow straight. Proper order too. Wouldn't mind chopping them both off if I had an excuse. Nothing but trouble anyway.

'The prize'. They slag me. 'What about the prize?'

Pretend I got rid of it long ago. No big deal. Gets them off my case. As if you'd want any of them fellas near you. Putting their big dirty hands on your privates. I keep all my bits well covered. Nothing for them to ogle. Not that there's a whole lot to put on display anyway, as coach says. He's right there. Ha, ha.

Coach and me, we speak the same language. He's a Dub too so he gets how I think. Knows how far to go with the slagging without going too far, mind. Though I'd never let on anyway. Suicide if you show any weakness. Means they'll come at you harder next time. That's what Rachel could never get. Stuck up she was. For all her leaving cert honours and college education. Hadn't a fucking clue. Little miss fucking perfect. I remember watching coach the first day she graced us with her presence. Couldn't fucking take his eyes off her boobs. She was well built, she was. I'll give her that. Like Britney Spears, only with a big head of long wavy brown hair and bigger boobs. Taller too. A college girl, we were told. She was friendly, like. Fucking eejit. Did she think we were all gonna be mates? Not fucking likely, not with us all looking to get on the team. This was war, this was. Nothing less.

Gas after the first match, though. Coach left the changing room and us girls started undressing behind our towels as usual. Miss perfect strips off. I mean completely bollock-naked. I was gobsmacked. She walks over, bold as brass and turns on the shower leaving the cubicle door open. I sat there, my mouth hanging open. My eyes was just stuck to her. I never seen a fully naked woman in my life. My Ma always dresses with her back to us or in the bathroom. Though there's eight of us we don't show our bodies at all. No fucking way. The only place I seen a near naked woman was in the magazine my brother Tommy had under his bed. But they looked awful; a slutty look in their eyes, big pouty lips and skimpy bits half-covering but not really covering their privates.

Rachel's body was the business, alright. Big muscly tanned shoulders, boobs sitting up staring you in the eye as if to say 'Fuck You', a curvy belly that was muscly too and massive tree trunk thighs, bony knees, calves like chicken fillets and ankles as thin as Mikey's wrists. Jesus, if I was a fella I wouldn't mind riding her. Then I felt all the girls looking at me. They look up to me, for leadership, like. I leapt out of my seat and slammed shut her cubicle door.

'A bit of privacy if you don't mind, Rachel. We're not a pack a lezzers round here. Don't know what you get up to in that college of yours but we cover up round here, we do'.

They seemed happy enough with that. Miss perfect didn't like it much, but didn't say nothing. I told coach about it after and he said he'd have a word with her. Coach hates lezzers. Gets real upset about them preying on the young girls.

She might have been a bit thick off the pitch but she was mighty on it. She went in hard. Never afraid. Generous too. Spread the ball around. Not a glory hunter, her. I'll give her that much. The girls liked that. When coach named the team that should have been the end of it. She made captain. I made vice, which was okay, like. I'm a scrawny little thing compared to her, short with skinny legs and a thin upper body. I've no weight behind me in a tackle. But I'm speedy and I'm real crafty on the set play. Never give up too. Like a terrier, I am. My left foot is always a surprise. But that wasn't the end of it, no. I think she got cocky, what with being captain and all. Lost the run of herself.

It was half time. We was going well. Well ahead of the opposition. Ran rings around them. The game was ours. Coach could see we was slackening off, getting sloppy, casual like. We was in the changing room, all sitting round, sipping bottles, leaning our backs against the wall. We wasn't really responding to what he was saying. We wasn't really reacting.

'Yez don't get it, do yez, ye stupid cunts. If yez don't stay hungry, stay in the game, those blind bitches'll take it back off yez'.

I could see Rachel's eyes twitch, her looking around the room. Thought maybe her sun cream was annoying her. The girls was mostly looking at their boots. This was the usual as far as they was concerned. This is what a coach has to do. Whatever language will get through to the stupid bitches. He was right. We couldn't afford to relax and get sloppy.

'Excuse me', says miss prissy.

That woke the girls up. They sat up then and looked sharp. Coach ignored her and went on with more of the same. Motivation talk, like. She wasn't having it.

'Excuse me, Coach. You can't talk to us like that'.

Coach turned to face her and stood over her. No one challenges coach. He said nothing. Just looked. Now, coach is one powerful man. He played in first division in the eighties. Coached professional in England and all. He's getting on, mind, what with the grey hair. But he looks after himself, he do. Always fit and tanned. Always gets into his boots, shorts and jersey for the warm-up then a suit for the match. Takes it real serious, like. This look of his started at her eyes, worked it's way down her body and slowly came back up again. He spoke real quiet.

'How dare you talk to me like that! I'm the boss 'round here. I makes the rules. No one's forcin' ya to be here. There's ten more waitin' for your place'.

He rips the armband off her and passes it to me, without lifting his eyes off Rachel.

'McGurl, you're captain for the rest o' the match'.

'Yes, coach, not a problem', says I.

Then Bagser comes into the changing room and calls time. Coach stands at the door as usual and we file out, slapping his hand as we go. I'm last so he walks out with me.

'Fuckin' cheek, coach. Who does she think she is? I don't care how good she is'.

'Fiddler, if I could take your head 'n screw it on the other fourteen pairs of shoulders, I'd do it'.

I ran onto that pitch fit to burst. We won that match of course. Nothing like a fight in the changing room to remind them this was to the death. I played a blinder. Piece of piss with that armband hugging my arm. Old miss prissy clogs made a balls of every pass. Coach had to sub her off in the end. That was the end of her. She was even crying leaving the changing room … fucking girl.

Shapeshifter

Sexual tension creates chaos yet you'd be lost without it. What does it mean when you feel it with a stranger? That your marriage is over? That you no longer love or desire your wife? Yet if you weren't unavailable would you feel it at all? What does it mean when you see your wife's senses prick, her eyelids open wider, her pupils dilate, the pulse in her neck start to bound? That the person across from her excites her, yes. But does that mean, like slicing a cake of a finite size, that there is less for you, that she feels less for you? Do you want her to stay with you while she dreams of him, make love with you fuelled by desire for him? And if she does stay, is that through a sense of duty to you or is it love? Is that insecurity or is it love?

Christopher stirs brown sugar crystals into his Americano, while his mind skirts the edges of these thoughts. He has the purplish tinge of an ex-drinker. He pings the spoon on the side of the cup, lays it on the saucer and waits. The sugar flitting against the porcelain sounds like ceramic wind-chimes wafting in a breeze. He checks his watch. His leather jacket creaks and the bunch of keys hanging from his jeans jangles.

He first met Elizabeth at a student party twenty years before. He remembers posters of Mohamed Ali and Che Guevara above two black bikes in the hallway. The sitting room was in semi-darkness, all the furniture removed apart from cushions scattered around the floor. The music boomed and a red bulb from a lamp in the corner cast a low light, outlining couples sitting and lying about the room.

In the kitchen, he leaned against the fridge in a lethargic haze, sipping his bottle of beer, his mind lolling after the frenzied fiddle reels earlier in the pub. He didn't know he was looking until she walked in. Widely spaced lazy brown eyes and tousled long hair. Tall but soft and curvy so he could imagine melting into her. Their eyes met and she smiled but not just at him.

'Five pounds entry to the first class carriage'. He said. She turned towards the sitting room. 'Hey, hang on, you can't go in there'.

'Why not?' Her voice was deep and resonant. '£10 entry, is it?'

'Worse. No fee but you'll come out changed. A different person'.

'Maybe I want to be a different person'.

'Right, so, I'll have a beer here waiting for you when your transformation is complete'.

Her lips parted and she floated into the sitting room. His thumb twisted his marriage band. He stared at the doorway.

'Have you any Harp?' her voice came from the other doorway.

He jumped then grabbed a bottle and opened by slamming it down on the edge of the table with his palm. He watched as she took a long draught of it.

'So, what brings you here? Are you a student?'

'Just finished finals today'.

She clinked bottles with his, looked at his ring and raised the bottle to her mouth for another slug.

'I see you're no student'. She said, looking around the room.

He ran his hands through his hair, caught. 'No'.

'You have transport?'

'Well, yes, of a kind'.

'Let's go, so'.

He unlocked the helmet from his motorbike and passed her the spare helmet from the pannier box.

His four months with her began that night. In all of that time there was always something beyond reach with Elizabeth. Some part of her that remained closed to him. As closed to him emotionally as she was open to him physically. He never knew whether it was that he had reached the limit of her. That he expected something from her she didn't have to give. Or maybe that there was something withheld. She was everything Martha wasn't.

At that time Martha was besotted with baby Katie. When it came to bathing, feeding, dressing and playing with the baby, she was the expert. He could do nothing right. He felt like a cuckold, an extra in his own home. One afternoon he finished early at the factory and arrived home with a cake and flowers. He crept into the house. As he walked up the carpeted stairs, placing each foot before transferring his weight onto it, he could hear her voice, half-whispering, half-singing and tender, so tender. The bedroom door was ajar. Martha was lying in bed naked with Katie in a nappy facing her. The baby's hands were holding Martha's cheeks and Martha was stroking the baby's face. Her voice had a softness he had never heard before. The look in her eyes naked, exposed. He slipped back down the stairs and left the house. After that the baby seemed to swell, gluttonously fattening on its monopoly. By the time he met Elizabeth, in Christopher's mind baby Katie had a head like a marshmallow with two buried currants for eyes and five ripples of flesh along each thigh.

Martha's interest in him centred upon his chances of promotion at the factory, a checklist of what else they could afford to buy for the baby and discussions on when it would be best for her next to conceive. A sister or brother for baby Katie. If she could see herself. Gone was the birdlike, tight-bodied working-class girl he had married. In her place was a shapeshifter in leggings and long T-shirts, originally loose but now at the limit of their elasticity.

For those four months Elizabeth's body was home to him. She liked clear space. In her bedroom there was nothing extra to her needs; no clutter, no frilly things, no fripperies of any kind. It was like sleeping in a model room in a design museum. He kept thinking spectators would walk in and pass comment, pointing at him, the only untidy object present. Unlike other women, Elizabeth had little interest in meals out, meeting friends or going to the pictures together. She was suspicious of being given flowers or presents of any kind. She preferred to make love without alcohol, an experience new to him. There was no taboo, judgement or fear. Just trust, curiosity and exploring each other's textures and contours, pleasures and limits. Bliss. She wanted from him what Martha didn't. She was even reluctant to talk.

Christopher waited, always expecting her to complain or to look for some return or commitment from the pleasure she gave him. It never happened. Free of the mundane habits of living together, they shared only sensuous touch. Words lacked the eloquence of their bodies. That summer they spent their stolen hours in her bedroom, on the sand dunes of deserted beaches or in the forest with a picnic.

Elizabeth's new job transferred her to London. If she was upset to be leaving him she didn't show it.

'Ten years from now', she asked the ceiling, beads of sweat on her forehead. 'Where will you be?'

He slid out of her, limp and rolled onto his back.

'You know where I'll be'.

'Oh?'

'I'll be precisely where I am now'.

'You don't know –'

'– Stuck in this town, married, with a wife as big as a house and an 11-year-old daughter playing catch-up'.

'You don't know for sure'.

'I can tell you where you'll be too'.

'Oh, can you now?'

'Married, I'd say, with one or two kids of your own'.

'How well you think you know me. Would you like to bet on it?'

They agreed to meet in ten years' time, on New Year's Eve in the Castle Hotel, Killiney.

It is now twenty years. Elizabeth walks past the coffee shop on the far side of the road so she can get a look at him before he sees her. That must be him sitting at the window, a shock of white hair in the place of his black curls. Lost in thought. She had tried googling him but no images came up apart from the court one, in which half his face was covered. The drizzle lightens; she closes her umbrella and crosses the street. She knows her figure is fuller than twenty years before yet she feels she has the same energy in her stride. Wearing a tailored navy trouser suit with an elaborate turquoise ceramic neck pendant and matching earrings, she stands for a moment with her back to a doorway next door to the coffee shop, looking out on the street view that he faces. A rogue memory returns to her.

Sitting on a train having just left him all those years before, her body freshly fucked and wanton. The mind has many veils to cover and uncover, she thinks. It has strange time locks too.

She grips the steel handle of the heavy glass door and wonders about the protocol on greeting. Handshake? Too formal. Kiss on the cheek? Too casual. Kiss on the lips? Too intimate. Hug? Too needy. Feck. Let him decide. Christopher stands up. He looks stunned and sheepish as he moves towards her. Handshake and the other hand on her shoulder. Friendly. But not a glimmer of the sexual. He has shrunk. She just realises what hopes she had harboured. Pity.

'Your lovely long hair', he says.

'Oh, yes', she says touching her forehead, 'it's easier to manage'.

She feels like she has damaged something belonging to him.

They fumble behind two small menus and she orders green tea and he another Americano. They look out the window and watch as a woman turns to her little boy and wags her index finger in his face. The boy doesn't react but looks past his mother at Elizabeth until his mother tugs him by the arm to walk on with her. His eyes are locked on Elizabeth to the last. Rain streams down the window.

'So how have you been anyway?' She asks.

'Good … things are better than …'

'Still married?'

'That's a good one, isn't it? Now that divorce is in, I wouldn't want it'.

Elizabeth's eyes dart from his face to her hands. Christopher shifts in his seat.

'But that's just me. My circumstances. Who am I to say?'

Elizabeth sits upright in her metal chair.

'Martha's doing very well'. She says.

'You wouldn't know her from the woman she was –'.

'We met at her exhibition in London, you know. Must have been five years ago. Justin was looking for a piece for the bank foyer and her paintings are wonderful'.

'That was just after the accident'.

'I particularly like her photography'.

'Katie was in hospital'.

'All those rock faces and canyons'.

'I thought she was going to leave me'.

'She must have done a study of geology'.

'That's when she told me'.

'Fascinating'.

'She knew'.

'And then there's the abstracts'.

'All that time she knew'.

'Her use of gold foil'.

'She just waited'.

'We discussed her ink drawings with her, too'.

'She's a bigger person than I ever could have been'.

'She really is talented'.

'The only way she'd stay is if I went to John of Gods and got myself sorted out'.

'– Of course you never met Justin, did you?'

'I was lucky to have a family to go back to, never mind a –'

'A fantastic chap. Loves the arts, theatre, painting, literature'.

The waitress arrives with the tray. She wipes the table with a blue J-cloth smelling of bleach, before placing their coffee and tea before them.

'Would yiz like anythin' else to go with that?'

'No, no thank you'. Elizabeth says in a tight voice.

'No problem'. She waddles back to the counter and picks up the phone to continue chatting.

After a few moments Christopher sits upright.

'So did you go to the Castle Hotel, in Killiney?'

She looks at him suspiciously.

'The ten year bet, remember? New Year's Eve?'

'Did you?' she says.

'I couldn't'.

Silence again. Christopher tries once more.

'You mentioned your husband, Justin'.

'Ex-husband'.

'Sorry. What happened?'

'Well. Let's see if I can I summarise it in less than three sentences'.

She sips her tea and returns the cup to its saucer.

'Okay. We met, we fucked, we loved, we married, then we split and now he's with someone else. One sentence, not bad'.

'Oh. I … I'm sorry'.

'I'm being rude now'.

'Look, it's okay, I – '

'I don't think this was a good idea. I'd better go'.

Elizabeth gets up and puts on her coat. Christopher stands also, his keys rattling and his hands hanging down empty.

'But I thought …'

'What? That we could pick up where we left off before?'

'Not like that'.

'Look, I'm sorry, this was a mistake'.

'I thought we could meet as … human beings … as people who shared something together in the –'

'I'm too old to pretend. I can't do this'.

Elizabeth lifts her scarf from the back of the chair, doubles it over and pushes the two free ends through a loop, drawing it up to her neck. She runs her hand around the back of her neck as if she still had long hair.

'There is no going back'.

'I never meant –'

'People or people's circumstances always change. Be happy with what we had and what you have now that you nearly lost'.

She holds out her hand and shakes his, realising she is keen to escape before there is time to change the deal. She pulls the heavy glass door open and steps out on to the street, now shiny after the rain.

The strange thing is, she thinks, that it seems she won the bet. Not so much because she is now divorced and childless, but because his life, though he is still married, has changed utterly. Whereas she feels close to being the person she was when they parted. She's not sure why she agreed to meet. What did she expect? What they did best together was horizontal and wordless. All their other interactions just preliminaries, things to be gotten out of the way. Drives, walks and conversations to get beyond. All to get to that glorious physicality, that sensate focus. Now he's a shadow of a man if ever there was one, hanging onto his wife's coat tails.

She enters a shopping centre, steps on the escalator and watches herself in the mirror as it carries her to the first floor. Relationships. So overrated. Together they had the only part of any value with none of the attendant tedium. Mad that the physical is regarded as base, when it's the pinnacle. The rest just wrangling; a contest for power played out over a lifetime together. Where life throws obstacles in each person's path to keep it interesting.

In the hairdressers she takes a seat at the sink. Her head basking in hot water, she relaxes into the assistant's hands.

'Day off today?'

'Yes, a day off'.

'Doing anything for the weekend?'

'No, no plans for the moment'.

Relieved when the questions end, she savours the rhythmic pressure on her scalp as a second shampoo is applied and afterwards a peach-smelling conditioner that is massaged in by the soft pads of the hairdresser's fingers. She presses her head into the hairdresser's hands like a Labrador straining for affection. Seated in front of a mirror having her hair cut, she watches the owner of the salon sitting nearby brushing her own hair out after a colouring, her movements similar to a cat washing its face.

After the cut and blow dry she makes her way back to her car. Walking past a row of houses with tidy hedges of copper beech, she runs her fingers along hedge tops as if reading Braille. When she reaches her car she realises she left her umbrella in the coffee shop. She doesn't go back.

Snagged

I wake up with the feeling of a warm wetness streaming out of me. Naked from the waist down. I feel cold, so cold. My hands reach to check. It must have been a dream. I'm sweating but my pyjamas are still on and I'm at home in my parents' house. On the ceiling a knot of wood is in the shape of a sharp-beaked bird, looking like he'd peck you.

Two weeks left in this place then I'm free. I can smell the rasher fat burning from here. It travels through the keyholes, under the doors and up through the floorboards. Best alarm clock ever made, according to Mammy. Once it's nine o'clock she wants all her guests up and out, fed and paid and gone from the place so she can get the rooms sorted before Mass. Well, so I can get the rooms sorted before Mass.

I remember the first summer she let me do the bedrooms, I'd just turned thirteen and got my monthlies. She showed me how everything had to be done. She had her method, you see, and you daren't stray from it.

First the ensuites, polishing the mirror with a squeaky rubbery cloth, cleaning both the sink plughole and the plug itself on both the topside and underside, with a small angled toothbrush. Using another brush on the base of the taps, especially underneath where the dirt collects, she said. Where dirt might collect if there was dirt and if it was let. The shower doors, polished inside and out. The jiff-soaked green scrub to the sink and shower enamel until the scratching sensation is gone and the cold surface is smooth to touch. Fake tan or hair dye, a divil to get off, bleach your only man. Every surface sprayed and wiped and the bathroom floor washed by hand, no other way to do it right, backing out the door on your hands and knees to finish.

Then the bed. Stripping the sheets, duvet cover and pillowslips. Making sure the crackly plastic protector is pulled well down over all the corners. There was no telling what state you'd find the bed in. Well, I lie, you could put money on it that an old couple or a settled married couple would be neat and tidy, the bed covers pulled over and pyjamas and nightie under the pillow and a book on the bedside table if they were staying a few nights. But if it was a singles' night-out in Galway, then man or woman it made no difference. There'd be clothes scattered everywhere; dresses, jeans and blouses at the door of the room, bras and socks down behind the bed, knickers and boxers stuck in the sheets or in the bed cover at the foot of the bed.

Mammy had me wear gloves.

'Never know what they get up to, love'. Her nose'd wrinkle up. 'And wouldn't want to know either'.

So at thirteen I was like a forensic investigator in my gloves, gathering all their clothes into one pile, stripping the soiled bed linen and dressing the beds again with fresh linen.

There's no kettle or coffee-making facility. 'Sure, can't they go out for that or have it before they come here'. Mammy said. 'This is no café. They're coming here to sleep, well …' So that was another cleaning job I was spared.

Once all the surfaces in the bedroom got a squirt and a wipe, hoovering was the last job. Then I'd open the window and sit on the bed and breathe in the fresh smell of weeds from the river. The sweat from the effort of hoovering would trickle down the side of my forehead and down the top of my stomach. I'd wait there, letting my heart slow until the breeze felt cold on my face. Then I'd gather all my bits and move onto the next room. That was my summer job from then on through school and college.

'And aren't you lucky to have a job at all?' Mammy used to say.

Very lucky, I'd be thinking, even luckier if I was getting paid.

The radio's turned up. Talky voices, must be *Sunday Miscellany*.

'How can you bear it?' Frances used to say, through her mane of hennaed hair. Her red dangling earrings clicking with each word, as if agreeing with her. 'I just have to get out of this country every summer. Don't know how you stick it'.

Not much point telling her I never had a choice. Family business, give and take. Or take and give. But we're quits now. She'd get so angry, Frances would. I think she enjoyed getting angry. The righteousness of it. Reacting to every injustice, or whatever she thought was unjust, students' rights, workers' rights, a woman's right to choose. Got her involved in the Rape Crisis Centre of all things. She even did their counselling training programme. Imagine going to her if it happened you. She wouldn't be able to listen to more than half the story before she'd blow up. She'd have to leave you midway to build a political campaign about it or write a strong article to the paper or go on radio or confront someone anyway. She'd have to do something, for sure. As though doing something is the solution to everything.

I snuggle down under the duvet for one last minute. I have my own duvet cover, pillowslips and sheets. Wouldn't want the guests using mine or me using theirs. I even wash them separately in our regular machine, not the industrial one. I breathe in expecting the pinecone smell of detergent. Instead it's the smell of wet anorak. Left too long in the machine again. Out of nowhere I remember his face. Brown eyes, high cheekbones. There was something weak about him. Must have been his teeth, stained since birth. I knew at the time there was something I didn't trust. Then I persuaded myself I shouldn't judge him on his teeth, poor lad couldn't help that.

It was the night after my finals and we'd met for a drink in a quiet pub just around the corner from my flat in Dublin. He didn't say much. Kept flipping beer mats and asking me lots of questions but didn't seem overly interested in my answers. Shifty, like. I'd decided anyway to leave after the one drink. But sure, after the one drink he had me. I woke up shivering in my own bed. My knickers below my knees, my socks still on, my blouse still on but open and my bra tangled around my neck. I thought I was dreaming. I looked around. My shoes were over at the door, my jeans thrown on the chair, my jumper at the foot of the bed. I sat up and felt the warm gush coming out of me, streaming down my legs onto the bed. The starchy smell of it. Unmistakable.

I jumped out of bed and tore what was left of my clothes off me and rushed into the shower. Oh I'd heard all Frances's stories alright, all the things you shouldn't do. But no way. No way was I going dressing with his greasy touch left on my flesh, his slime inside me. No way was I going telling this story to anyone else. Bad enough that it happened without everyone hearing about it and finding out what an eejit I was to have been taken in. Bad enough that it went this far. No. It was stopping here.

I sat down in the shower and angled my hips so the water rained down inside me, washing him out of me. Cleaning me of his filth. My fingers searched all over my body wondering where he had been. I had to take it back. I rubbed my forehead and cheeks and neck, soaping and rinsing, soaping and rinsing. Then my chest and stomach and legs. Scrubbing and scrubbing. I kept thinking of other parts of me he might have reached. What about my ears? What about my mouth? I wasn't there. How could I know? Nothing for it but to presume the worst. Every part of me I scrubbed, even poking soap into my backside and crouching on the floor of the shower for the water to pour inside to rinse it out.

Once I was wrapped up in towels I found a pair of gloves I'd used for highlights and stuffed all the bed linen and all the clothes I'd worn into a black plastic disposal bag.

I put on a tracksuit and hoodie and packed up a week early. I was down in Galway before dark that night with nothing in my stomach except the morning-after-pill I'd washed down with a slug of water. That was three months ago.

'Sandra!' Mammy again, now at the foot of the stairs. 'Get up. It's nine thirty'.

I'm up like a shot, shower and dress and report for duty in the kitchen. Mammy scoops a dozen rashers off the skillet onto a dish, covers it and places it in the warming oven. She rests the greasy end of the slice on a side plate and returns the oven gloves to the hook on the wall. No point trying to have my own breakfast before the guests are done because she won't leave me in peace. So I wait. She washes her hands and dries them with a paper towel, snatching it from hand to hand as if trying to get gum off her palms. Then she squirts hand cream onto one palm and works it into her fingers, drawing each of her rings forwards to reach the skin behind them. She turns to me, stares at me and then seems to see me.

'Find out if that Murray family want three full Irish again today, would you?'

'Is Dad up?'

Her chin drops and her lips flatten out. I follow her glance out the window to the caravan. The curtains are still pulled. She crosses her freckled arms and stares at me.

'Okay, okay. The Murray family'.

When I return she is standing in front of the small mirror rearranging the combs in her hair. Dad walks in the back door.

'Morning all'. He says.

'Well?' she says, looking at me.

'Three full Irish' I say. 'Have you just the one more after?'

'Any breakfast going?' Dad says.

'Ye're great for the questions, the pair of ye. Must be your big brains, needing to suck up all that information'.

She melts a knob of butter on the skillet, spreading it with the tip of the slice. The scratch of metal on metal. I start to unload the dishwasher.

'Brenda?' he says. 'Is there any cooked breakfast going?'

I'm not getting caught in this one. It's his third time since Christmas.

'Just the one yank left', she says. 'Still asleep. If he doesn't rise soon he can forget breakfast'. She cracks three eggs onto the skillet and scoops oil over the top. I watch as the orange yolk films slowly to white.

'So when'll the conferring be?' she asks, eyeing the eggs.

'Sometime in September, I'd say'.

'Brenda?' Dad's standing next to her.

She covers the eggs with a lid, turns off the hob and pivots around to me.

'Come out to the line with me and help me bring in those duvet covers before that shower of rain catches them'.

At the line we unpeg the white sheets and duvet covers and it starts to rain so we drape them over our shoulders and hurry in, looking like two red-faced Roman senators. Dad hasn't moved.

She stands in front of him and looks at him like you'd eye an extinct animal you never liked in a glass display case.

'I did like Chris's mother's dress last night, I must say'. She says. 'That woman has style'.

Dad's about to speak when she cuts in.

'But do you know what really galls me, Sandra?'

She lifts a sheet, snaps it out and holds it by both corners. I reach for the opposite corners and bring them to her. She opens her fingers to receive them.

'What really galls me is having to put up with someone who's weak. Someone who has no word'. I bring the lower half of the sheet up to her. 'A lily-livered liar'.

She folds it again and lays it on the pile for ironing.

'What did I do?' says Dad, now seated at the table.

She presses both her hands flat on the centre of the sheet, leaning in with her weight, moving her hands from the middle to the edges, flattening the creases.

'I liked Mrs. Daly's outfit too'. I say. 'She has the height to wear it'.

'Oh, she's trailing after her husband, she is. Now that man can carry a suit, no question'. She busies herself at the hob again.

'Tell me what I –'

'Dad –'

'– Oh, don't waste your breath, Sandra. He's only looking for notice'.

She places four slices of brown bread in the toaster and hands me the tray loaded with the three cooked breakfasts.

When I return from the dining room, he's pouring milk on his cereal and she's lost in a cloud of steam over the ironing machine. He starts to suck cereal off his spoon and she jerks back the ironing cover, reaches to turn up the Irish reels on the radio then returns to her ironing.

Sometimes I wonder what it's like when I'm not here. Maybe they put this show on for my benefit and they're harmonious in my absence. As if they have to show me they need me here. Or maybe they really do need me here. Whichever way it is, it makes no odds. I'm gone. Today she's in a fit because he was drinking again last night. But there are days when he doesn't drink and she's equally raging. I bring my cereal to the table and sit down across from him.

'I was thinking, Sandra', she says. Once the focus is off him then she turns it on me. We are her two main settings. I wait her out.

'Well, I was surprised, I have to say'. She continues. 'Seemed kinda sudden'.

'Sudden?'

'Your engagement'.

'Sandra knows Chris this long time, Brenda', Dad pipes up.

The withering look she reserves for him alone is delivered and he returns his attention to his mug of tea. After years of watching them, what's surprising isn't that she maintains this consistent level of hostility but that he expects her to be different. As though he's clutching onto his original impression of her and no hostility expressed by her will ever change that.

I finish my cereal and stand by the kettle waiting for it to boil.

She's no fool. It surprised me too, going out with Chris again, getting engaged. It's not what I expected either. We had parted ways after the Leaving cert, me off to study Social Work in Dublin, him staying on in Galway to study Science. I'd had a number of boyfriends since, most of them wild and carefree, polar opposites to Chris.

I felt very strange when I first moved back. I stayed in, did my work in the B&B and went for walks by the lake. I was jumpy, nervous, couldn't concentrate for long. I'd start laughing at something stupid, like the dog trying to hump the cushion and I'd finish up crying. I'd get upset about things that didn't matter, like when one of the kittens was born dead.

One day I was driving across town from collecting stuff at the wholesalers when I saw this old man teetering. He wasn't drunk. You could tell. He would have been seventy or eighty years old. All dressed up for his day out in Galway, his good suit and woollen coat over, wearing his best hat and he was walking along the street and he started drifting to one side and I was sitting in traffic and all the cars around me, everyone was watching him and no one was going to do anything and I couldn't bear it. I drove my car up onto the wide pavement and I parked and grabbed him just before he went down and I saved his head from hitting the ground and I sat with him and I asked him was he okay and he said he wasn't sure and I asked him where he lived and he said he'd just come out of hospital so I helped him into the back of my car and I drove him to Casualty where the nurse took him in on a wheelchair. And I looked around and wondered, does no one care? This old man and no one belonging to him with him, does no one but me care? I had to wait in the Dunnes car park for my crying to stop before I could go on home.

So I was out walking by the lake one afternoon and I heard this strange noise from a duck and I looked and out in a boat was a man and a boy. A duck seemed to have got snagged in their fishing line and they were following it to the bank. As they got closer I saw it was Chris with his younger brother. He was teaching him how to fish. The poor duck had the hook stuck in his head and the young lad was crying, thinking he'd killed it.

I caught the rope and tied their boat to the mooring and helped the young lad in. Chris managed to catch the duck and calm it and I held its wings down while he snipped one end off the hook and fed the metal through the wound to free it, without ripping any more of the its flesh.

'There now, Sandra, it's out, you can let him off, he's grand'.

I didn't want to let the duck go. I started crying. Chris took the duck from my hands, smoothened over the feathers where it had been cut, placed it on the water and it swam away. The young lad started laughing at me crying and then I started laughing. We must have looked a right pair. Chris just stared at me. This was not the Sandra he went out with at school. She had her mother's mettle, afraid of nothing. She could look after herself. He put his arm around me and hugged me and it took all my will not to cry again and I wasn't able to move out of his hug and somehow he knew that. I went back in the boat with them as far as the pier in the quiet of the evening. The quiet of no one talking and the boat creaking with each stroke and the fresh water slapping against the sides and the click and slide of the young lad's rod casting and reeling in. Each of those sounds had a comfort in them. Chris asked me would I join them again and we ended up passing the summer afternoons together out on that lake. I can't say if it was him or the boat or the lake but part of me knew that this was what I needed. Then in August the young lad went on a summer camp so it was just me and Chris and lots of quiet.

'I suppose it seems that way all right'. I say to my mother. 'Sudden, like. But it's not really. We've been together all summer'. I pour boiling water into my mug and the coffee granules melt.

I feel the cold on my leg again as if I'm naked.

'And he's a good man'.

My blouse is open and pulled to one side digging into my armpit.

'We get on great together'.

The underwire from my bra is cutting into my neck and I feel a pulsing pressure in my forehead.

'He's my best friend. I trust him'.

My hands are freezing. I can't move my arms or legs. A cold black eel slithers up my leg. I can't move away. I can't stop him. He's between my legs, he's inside me. He tunnels through me and comes out my mouth. He slides around my neck ringing it in three bands so I can't breathe and my eyes bulge and my head feels like it'll burst. He slips over my breasts first circling each, then both in a figure of eight then he burrows into the bed to come around my back looping my chest and squeezing and squeezing.

They're both standing in front of me, looking worried.

'What?' I say.

'Sit down, love. Sit down'. She says. 'You're covered in sweat'.

He pulls over a chair and I sit down.

'Are you okay?' he says.

'Yeah, course. Why wouldn't I be?'

Antemortem

Carthage woke at dawn on the day of his death. He showered then dry-shaved by touch. He reheated porridge and sat out on the back step to eat it. He was a tall man with a mop of raven-black hair, a lantern jaw and a wiry frame.

'A dishwasher is a beautiful thing', he whispered, as he reached in to unclip both rotating arms. He ran the tap water through the central hole and watched the spouts of water coming out each end, like a child spilling water out of its mouth after punching both cheeks. He rinsed the filter then clicked it back into place, flush. He had had a similar ritual with the miners' lamps he polished in Arigna as a child. As he worked, time stood still and his movements slowed, so it was more of a caress than a duty.

He left the house and walked to the tube station where he bought *The Roscommon Herald*. He got off at Ealing and made his way to the hospital.

'Howya Carthage? Any news from home?' Josie, a matronly Cork woman smelling of Juicy Fruit, greeted him in the pathology office.

Carthage smiled his crinkly smile, his conversation dodger, and kept walking. Once changed into blue scrubs, he reviewed the morning's list; two BIDs, one hanging and infant twins.

He moved to the first body brought in dead and set to work. Each time he peeled back the layers of a body he moved quickly. Within each there was something the pathologist wanted him to find: the clot lodged in a heart or brain artery, the broken neck vertebra of a hanging victim, waterlogged lungs in a suspected drowning, or the puncture-wound tracking a knife's insertion through the rib space, through the sack around the heart, reaching its inner silken lining. These were not what Carthage was looking for. As he weighed the heart, lungs and brain and noted his findings, his pace slowed. Stephanie walked past the glass-block wall often, click clack, click clack. That's all I need, he thought, an attractive woman. They're a bloody curse.

He moved on to the twins. They were wrapped together in an orange fleece blanket. Reflexively he put his little finger inside each of the tiny fists, as though they would grip him back. They were dressed in yellow woollen hand-knitted suits with buttons of different plastic fruits, little pixie hats with silver bells on them and laced bootees. He undressed them carefully and folded their clothes and unsoiled nappies on a chair. Then he lifted their fleece blanket, folded it and pushed his face into it and breathed it in. Other people's homes and the smells that belong there. He laid the twins out like two pinned butterflies and carefully made the incisions so the pathologist could get to work. With infants you had to take great care. Their bodies were held and hugged to the last before being placed in the coffin.

Next he moved onto the hanging. He looked into the man's face. Whatever had driven him to it was long gone. He looked mellow, as though he might stretch, take a deep breath and at any moment shout, 'Jesus, what's keeping ye? Will ye get a move on?'

Carthage took down the drill and started to bore the dead man's skull. He removed the brain and weighed it, then moved on to open the chest and abdomen. The pathologists wore masks while they worked. Carthage didn't bother, the smell of animal or human innards of no consequence to him.

Through the open window he smelled cigarette smoke and stopped working. Stripping off his gloves and apron and washing his hands, he remembered the two things about Nasreen he loved most: the sweet thread of tobacco that his tongue invariably found in some crevice of his mouth after leaving her, and the soft curve at the top of her leg where her thigh muscle attached to her hip bone. A small pad of flesh quivered there when she moved. He loved to rest his head on her stomach and run his fingertips over where firm muscle met soft flesh. Lying there felt like home.

He walked down the corridor, past the open door of the packed staff room. In the hallway the coffee machine spat an acrid black liquid into a beige plastic cup. He took it outside and lit up. He nodded at Sanjeet, a small man in his sixties with pianist's hands and sad eyes, who smoked in silence. They could have been outside a church in Mohill on a warm spring Sunday, studiously ignoring the priest's request, audible through the packed open door, to show each other the sign of peace.

Each day Carthage opened his lunchbox in the empty staff room and unwrapped the same piece of tinfoil with his sandwich inside. Lunch today was two slices of soda bread with lumps of smoked ham, scallions and mayonnaise. Once finished he sauntered away, biting on a red apple as the others arrived. He walked across the hospital football pitch into the woods and lay on a mossy bank beside a stream. He looked up at the sun through the leaves. Nasreen smelt of popcorn. It wasn't from her face cream or make-up. He had checked them. It was from deep inside her. He could find it in her exhaled air as she lay asleep beside him and he moved in close to rebreathe her. It wafted from her pores in the heat. He looked down at the shadows made by the leaves on his hands. They were like shadows that move across the bottom of the wash-basin when suds float across the surface. This reminded him of a cloud's shadow tacking along the side of Ben Bulben on a windy day.

He left the woods and detoured to Davy's bookies before returning to the lab.

'Hello Irish, what can I do you for?' Pat grinned, scratching his sparse ginger beard.

'Two pound each way on Birch Rider. The four o'clock'.

Pat took the money and gave him his docket. He was a plump man with fish-like blue eyes and long blond lashes.

'Will you be in Flanagan's for one later? Marty's coming down for the night'.

'Maybe I will'.

'We'll be there after nine'.

'See you so'.

Carthage spent the afternoon working on sections of the organs he had removed, taking slices at angles that best showed the cause of death. Stephanie click-clacked in and out, transferring specimens for staining to the lab upstairs. She was a buxom woman in her late thirties, the kind who assaults the senses with strong perfume and an extra loud voice even when standing closeby. She reminded him she was having a hen party that night after work. The more she crowded Carthage, the more he withdrew, to the point that now he didn't meet eye contact or reply.

His final job that day with Sanjeet was to stitch closed the rib cages, chests, abdomens and skulls as neatly as possible. At five o'clock they went for their last cigarette of the day. Sanjeet's long toes combed the grass.

'Two years I have left here in this dung hole. My wife, she loves it. But in my heart I am still in Thakor. Everyday my mind is visiting the market and breathing in the curries along with the putrid smells. Two more years, if God is willing'. The two men's eyes met and held, then Carthage looked away.

He bought two fillet steaks, a head of white cabbage and new potatoes. The bus dropped him to Flanagan's Pub. He climbed the metal stairs at the side of the building, the tips of his shoes ting-tinging and the plastic food bag swishing against the metal railing. He rang the doorbell. After a few minutes he put a key in the lock and let himself in. The apartment was dark, smelling of wine and dope. He opened the curtains and the windows. In the kitchen he set the cabbage and potatoes boiling, then washed the frying pan, dried it and spilled rock salt onto it laying the two steaks on top. Tariq lay sprawled on the bed, his face obscured by his long hair. A beam of light from the evening sun lit up one buttock and a thin blackhaired leg. Carthage bent over, kissed him on the back of his neck, slapping the bare buttock.

Tariq rolled around surprised and wiped saliva from his chin. His eyes were blood shot. In the kitchen Carthage whistled while listening to the racing news on Radio 1. Then he switched it off and tuned in to Tariq singing in the shower.

Flanagans was a comfortable pub until the new owners replaced the Formica and bubbled glass. Now it looked like a stage set for the Abbey. Despite this, the regulars continued to drink there.

Mike, a red-faced brickie with a fading sunburn line on his neck and carrots for fingers, was seated at the bar with his pint and chaser. He regaled Tariq, who was working behind the bar, with his victorious stories, the theme always his ingenuity, the great man he was in fooling the Englishman.

Tariq's attention was on the function room at the back where screams of laughter and singing were heard each time the door opened. Igor and his two Ukrainian friends sat outside like sentries. At the other end of the bar, two young Bengali men dressed in suits were deep in conversation. Carthage was smoking, leaning against the wall while Pat and Marty played pool. The pool cue was like a talking stick; each took their turn to speak before taking a shot. Marty was telling a story about an M1 motorway rescue call-out he had done that day.

'So he says to me, "You're rippin' us off mate, that's double you are chargin' for petrol". So I says, I'm not your mate. Take it or leave it. I'm not here for the good o'me health. Like it or lump it. Fuckin' Pakis'.

'What did he say to that?' Pat grinned.

'Well, he went back to the car. You shoulda seen it. His wife, all meek, like, but his mother, she bawled him out of it. He paid in the end, though. No choice. What do they expect? Everythin' for nothin'?'

Carthage watched Tariq serve pints to the two young men. When they took their seats again Tariq caught his eye and Carthage looked away.

The function room door opened and women teetered out. They wore pink hair bands bearing fluffy antennae and flashing lights.

Josie marched to the middle of the room and set down a high stool.

'Right. It's Stephanie's last time in here a single woman so we'll have a kiss, a nice orderly kiss now, from every man in the room. Form a queue lads'.

Clad in a bright red dress with a plunging neckline, Stephanie swaggered over to the stool. Her bangles jingled when she perched coquettishly on the edge of the stool. Her face dropped as Mike staggered over to her. He wiped both hands on his trousers, and his mouth with his sleeve. He approached her stealthily like a man might approach a wild dog. She pointedly turned her head to one side to receive his kiss.

Next up was Pat; he walked shyly towards her, placed a hand on each shoulder and kissed her on both cheeks.

'I wish you the very best. I'm sorry we're losin' ya to a Latvian'.

'He's Russian'.

'Sure they're much of a muchness'.

Igor straightened up in his seat, craning to hear what was being said. Marty sauntered up to Stephanie and pulled her out for a quick jig around the room. Igor stood and ran his hands through his short spiked hair. Marty winked at him as they passed. Josie announced a break in the proceedings and the women went to the bar for another drink.

Stephanie linked Carthage's arm as he leaned on the bar.

'So now you've missed your chance with me'.

He disengaged and took a deep draw on his pint.

'How do you feel about that?'

He walked away.

'Just who do you think ya are, Mr God Almighty?' She shouted after him. 'I was talking to you. Don't just walk away when I'm talkin' to ya. It's rude'.

Her shoulder strap had slipped and Igor moved swiftly to her side.

'Is this man a problem?'

'Naah. Feck him'. She turned back to Josie.

Carthage took up the pool cue and continued to play, ignoring Igor. Josie steered Stephanie back to her stool.

'Last chance, lads, we'll have three more kisses for the lovely Stephanie before she is lost forever into marriage'.

Igor remained standing at the bar, his pint in his hand and his hooded eyes casing the room. The two young Bengali men stood and approached Stephanie. The first, in an ill-fitting suit and plastic shoes, pecked her cheek and hurried back to his seat. His friend in a linen suit, smelling of strong aftershave, kissed her on the lips and his right hand brushed briefly against her breast. She craned into the kiss. Igor placed his pint on the bar and bounded over. He grabbed his arm, twisted it then kicked him to the floor and started to kick him in the face and stomach. Stephanie staggered back, fascinated in a disconnected way. Carthage intervened,

'Enough. Back off. He's only a kid'.

'Lads, lads, now lets all calm down'. Josie stepped between the two men, placing a hand on each arm. They stared at each other, nostrils flaring. 'It's over. Back to your seats'.

Igor's two friends accompanied him back to his seat and to a fresh pint. Carthage and Josie helped the young man off the floor. He retrieved his glasses and dusted down his clothes. His left eye was swollen and he had a cut lip. He scurried out of the bar with his friend.

The smell of wet leaves filled the room as Tariq opened the back door to change a keg. The hen party, now just five women, sat around a table and the bar hushed as each took turns to sing songs of love and loss. Igor and his friends looked sombre, each alone in his world.

At the end of Josie's song, Tariq turned up the lights and opened the front door. The street was shiny after a shower.

Stephanie stood at the door, hugging each of her friends as they left. Carthage sat at the end of the bar, watching

Tariq clear up. Igor came out of the mens' toilets as Stephanie taunted,

'I never got my kiss from you, Carthage'.

Carthage looked straight at her.

'Will you not wish me luck?'

'Good luck'.

He turned back to the bar. Igor exchanged looks with his two friends and they left with Stephanie. Carthage swept the lounge as Tariq put glasses into the machine. Once finished he switched off the lights. They left by the front door.

Carthage heard a dull thud behind him as he placed his foot on the first step of the metal stairway. When he looked around Tariq was on the ground being kicked by two men. He lunged to punch the nearest when he felt a blow to the side of his head. He heard a high-pitched hissing sound like a burst mains pipe as his body folded to the ground. Blood pumped from the severed artery, filling the space, expanding to compress his soft brain against the hard casing of his skull. The blood clot grew from the size of a bean to a tennis ball.

He was sleeping curled up beside Nasreen, her head tucked under his chin, her shoulders against his chest, her back fitting the curve of his stomach, her buttocks against his groin, his member between her legs, at the point of entry, her hips encased by his hands, her legs draped like a rug across his, her feet like two mackerel rolled in newspaper, between both of his. She was so cold, he couldn't warm her. He could hear Tariq calling him as a red canopy over the bed slowly closed them in. He wasn't leaving her, not now. The bed slowly lowered down a mine shaft into a cold damp pit.

About the Author

Aideen Henry writes short fiction, drama and poetry. Her short stories, 'Saibh' and 'Idling', were shortlisted for the Francis MacManus Award in 2011 and 2012. 'Idling' was published in *The Dublin Review* in 2012. She has contributed short stories to three published collections of the Atlantis Collective. Her three one-act plays were staged at NUI, Galway and the Galway Theatre Festival. Her debut poetry collection, *Hands Moving at the Speed of Falling Snow,* was published by Salmon Poetry in 2010 and that year she was shortlisted for the Emerging Poetry Section of the Hennessy XO Literary Awards. *Hugging Thistles* is her debut collection of short stories.